S0-AFV-407

Carrie shivered.

"This is the most depressing conversation I've ever had."

Billy's arm tightened around her. "It would be a lot more depressing if you actually were sick." He gently reached up and pushed a lock of hair off of Carrie's face. "I guess I'd take care of you," Billy said slowly. He leaned over and gave her a soft kiss.

"And I'd take care of you," Carrie replied. "But how can someone live knowing they're going to die . . ."

The SUNSET ISLAND series
by Cherie Bennett

Sunset Island
Sunset Kiss
Sunset Dreams
Sunset Farewell
Sunset Reunion
Sunset Secrets
Sunset Heat
Sunset Promises
Sunset Scandal
Sunset Whispers
Sunset Paradise
Sunset Surf
Sunset Deceptions
Sunset on the Road
Sunset Embrace
Sunset Wishes
Sunset Touch
Sunset Wedding
Sunset Glitter
Sunset Stranger
Sunset Heart

Also created by Cherie Bennett

Sunset After Dark
Sunset After Midnight
Sunset After Hours

Sunset Heart

CHERIE BENNETT

Sunset™ Island

SPLASH™

A BERKLEY / SPLASH BOOK

If you purchased this book without a cover, you should be aware that this book is stolen property. It was reported as "unsold and destroyed" to the publisher, and neither the author nor the publisher has received any payment for this "stripped book."

SUNSET HEART is an original publication of
The Berkley Publishing Group.
This work has never appeared before in book form.

SUNSET HEART

A Berkley Book / published by arrangement with
General Licensing Company, Inc.

PRINTING HISTORY
Berkley edition / April 1994

All rights reserved.
Copyright © 1994 by General Licensing Company, Inc.
Cover art copyright © 1994 by General Licensing Company, Inc.
This book may not be reproduced in whole or in part,
by mimeograph or any other means, without permission.
For information address: General Licensing Company, Inc.,
24 West 25th Street, New York, New York 10010.

A GLC BOOK

Splash and *Sunset Island* are trademarks belonging to
General Licensing Company, Inc.

ISBN: 0-425-14183-7

BERKLEY®
Berkley Books are published by
The Berkley Publishing Group,
200 Madison Avenue, New York, New York 10016.
BERKLEY and the "B" design
are trademarks belonging to Berkley Publishing Corporation.

PRINTED IN THE UNITED STATES OF AMERICA

10 9 8 7 6 5 4 3 2 1

For you know who

ONE

"Tell me every detail," Samantha Bridges insisted as she resettled her John Lennon-style sunglasses on her nose. "Don't leave anything out."

"How would you know if I did?" joked her friend Carrie Alden, who was sprawled out on the sand next to Sam.

"I'd know," Sam replied.

"She has radar for that sort of thing," their friend Emma Cresswell commented archly, turning over to sun her back.

"So, spill your guts!" Sam commanded. "There's no one else around to hear!"

"Except about three thousand other people," Carrie observed, looking up and down the crowded stretch of beach on

Sunset Island where the three girls were spending their Saturday afternoon. It was an absolutely magnificent day on the southern Maine coast, without a cloud in the sky. There was some sort of kite-flying festival going on at the south end of the beach, and all sorts of colorful kites filled the sky.

"Look at that one!" Carrie cried, pointing to one kite that looked like a flying red-and-white squid, replete with five long tentacle-tails swooping and soaring.

"You're changing the subject!" Sam scolded as she shook her long red hair off her shoulders.

"Carrie doesn't have to tell you about her date with Billy unless she really wants to," Emma said, settling her head into the crook of her elbow.

"Of course she does," Sam insisted. "It's some best-friend rule kind of thing."

"Okay, okay." Carrie laughed. "I give up. But get me a soda first."

Sam reached into the mini-cooler they had brought to the beach with them and took out three bottles of flavored seltzer.

"Cherry okay?" she asked Carrie. Carrie nodded.

"You want one, Em?"

"Okay," Emma answered. "I'm a little hot."

"No," Sam remarked. "*Carrie* was a little hot. Last night. With Billy. Now, give me dirt!"

Carrie laughed. "You are too much, Sam."

"Hey, check out the major hunk playing Frisbee in the surf over there!" Sam cried, her attention momentarily diverted from prying juicy stories out of Carrie.

Carrie grinned. *That is just so Sam,* she thought to herself. *I still can't believe that Sam, Emma, and I are here together on the island for the second summer in a row! Sam may be impossible, and Emma may be the most perfect person ever born, but they are the greatest friends in the world!*

Carrie had met Sam and Emma more than a year before at the International Au Pair Convention in New York City. And all three of them were lucky enough to get jobs working as au pairs for families who summered on fabulous Sunset Island, the world-famous summer resort island located at the far reaches of Casco Bay off the coast of Portland, Maine.

Carrie, in fact, had been hired by rock-and-roll legend Graham Perry Templeton and his wife Claudia to take care of their thirteen-year-old son Ian and their five-year-old daughter Chloe. The Templetons lived in an incredible house, and Carrie still couldn't believe her luck in getting hired by them.

Too bad I like jazz more than I like rock, she thought. *But they're a great couple to work for! Almost as great as it is being friends with Sam and Emma. Who would ever think that Emma Cresswell, heiress to the huge Cresswell fortune, and the most cultured and worldly person I've ever met, would turn out to be my best friend? And that my other best friend would be a wild, outrageous, tall, red-headed dancer from Kansas who never met an adventure she didn't want to try?*

The most amazing thing of all was that Carrie, who had completed her freshman year at Yale and wanted to be a photojournalist, Emma, who had done her first year at Goucher College in Maryland, and Sam, who had quit Kansas State University to dance at Disney World (and then got fired for being "too original"!), were all back at Sunset Island for their second summer in a row.

Carrie looked over at Emma as Emma pulled some sunscreen out of her beach-bag. *Anyone could tell how different we are just by looking at our bathing suits,* Carrie realized. *Emma has on a perfect, white one-piece suit with high-cut legs and a halter neck, Sam has on the world's tiniest hot-pink bikini with fringe, and I've got on my black one-piece.*

"Tell me that, on a scale of one to ten, that guy isn't a serious eleven," Sam said, squinting at the Frisbee-throwing Adonis.

"Oops," Emma said, "don't look now, but the object of your lust has a girl-friend." Emma tilted her head at a cute girl in a thong-backed bikini, who was running down the beach toward the guy.

"Figures." Sam snorted. "Oh well, we know cuter guys than him, anyway."

Carrie laughed. *The cutest guy I know is Billy Sampson, the one and only true love of my life. He's the lead singer of Flirting with Danger, and the coolest, smartest, funniest, kindest, sexiest guy I've ever met. Not that I'm biased!*

"So, forget the awesome surfer dude," Sam joked, turning back to Carrie. "We await shocking details about your date with Billy."

"Well," Carrie began, hugging her knees to her chest, "we had the most romantic dinner together last night on the terrace at the Sunset Inn."

"Yeah, yeah, yeah," Sam said. "But what I care about is the after-dinner aerobic activities."

"You're terrible!" Emma said. "It sounds like a wonderfully romantic dinner!"

"It was," Carrie agreed blissfully.

"Yeah, so go on," Sam coaxed, taking a slug of her soda.

"We went for a walk on the beach," Carrie continued.

"And it was so gorgeous last night." Emma sighed.

"*Billy* was so gorgeous last night, huh?"

Sam translated. "Carrie wasn't looking at the sky." She turned to Carrie. "So, how far did you go?"

Carrie blushed slightly. "This is personal," she said.

"That's why I'm asking," Sam explained patiently.

"Well . . . we went pretty far," Carrie admitted.

"How far?" Sam demanded.

Emma swatted Sam on the arm. "Stop it!"

"I can't help it!" Sam defended herself. "I have no love life! I have to live vicariously!" She edged closer to Carrie. "So, go on."

"We stopped at the far end of the beach," Carrie said, "and Billy had brought a blanket with him, and—"

"Get down, Carrie!" Sam yelped. "You finally went—"

"Nope," Carrie interrupted. "Believe me, one side of me wanted to, and the other side—"

"Wasn't sure." Emma completed the sentence for her. "I can understand that."

"You are driving me nuts with this 'I'm not sure' stuff!" Sam cried.

"Oh, believe me, my body is sure," Carrie admitted. "I think it's mostly because of the AIDS test. Hey, pass me the sunscreen, huh?"

Sam passed the bottle over to Carrie.

"But you and Billy talked about him taking an AIDS test," Emma recalled. "I thought he said he would."

"Yeah," Sam added.

"Well, he did say that," Carrie agreed, spreading the sunscreen on her shoulders. "But he hasn't done it yet. And I don't think I should even consider having sex with him until he takes the test and we get the results."

"That makes sense," Emma said.

"Well, I suppose it's logical," Sam agreed, "but it sure isn't romantic."

"Sam, romance is not worth dying for," Carrie said.

"Oh, come on," Sam chided Carrie. "Billy with AIDS? Gimme a break!"

"Anyone can get AIDS, even straight people who don't do drugs," Carrie said.

8

"But Billy is totally true to you!" Sam cried.

"Okay," Carrie agreed, "but how about any girl he had sex with before we even met? He could be carrying the virus and not even know it!"

"But he's straight and he doesn't shoot drugs—" Sam began.

"So?" Emma said. "That doesn't make him immune. What if he once had a girlfriend who shot drugs? Or what if he once had a girlfriend who once had a boyfriend who slept around? Or—"

"I get your point," Sam said.

"And even the AIDS test isn't foolproof," Emma added. "I read that somewhere."

"Me, too," Carrie said. "I read that it can take six months or more for the virus to show itself."

"So what did you decide?" Emma asked cautiously.

"We're going to talk about it again," Carrie explained. "This is such a hassle!"

"Yeah," Sam said, "I heard that back in the sixties and seventies people just did it and didn't have to worry about dying."

"I'm not sure that was so great, either," Emma commented, taking a big swig of her soda.

Sam and Carrie looked at her.

"Who knows?" Emma said with a shrug. "Maybe they didn't take sex seriously *enough*."

You might be right, Carrie thought. *I'm not sure that because you can die now from getting AIDS means that before AIDS it was so great to have sex without even being in a committed relationship. I bet lots of people got hurt that way.*

"So listen," Sam instructed Carrie, "get back to us and let us know what you decide."

"Is that an order?" Carrie asked ruefully.

"No," Sam replied solemnly. "But thanks for asking!"

After Carrie had dinner that night with Claudia, Ian, and Chloe Templeton (Graham was working late at the studio), Chloe went into the family room to play Nintendo. As they had discussed before, Carrie took the opportunity to enlist

Claudia and Ian in a project she had to do for the upcoming semester at Yale.

For her photojournalism class, Carrie had gotten the summer assignment to put together a portfolio of her twenty best photographs that told a story, and then to write captions for each of them. While Carrie had assembled literally hundreds of prints over the last couple of summers, she'd done nothing to get her portfolio project together.

"This one's good!" Ian exclaimed, digging to the bottom of a stack of photos to pick one out and hold it up to Carrie for her approval.

"Ian," Claudia laughed, "no self-serving photo selection allowed."

Ian had plucked out a photo that Carrie had taken of Ian and his industrial-music band, Lord Whitehead and the Zit People. The "music" consisted of the band members banging on hulked-out appliances and industrial equipment with metal pipes, while chanting along to pre-recorded cassettes. To Carrie, the band's sound was somewhere between awful and a nightmare. Becky and Allie Jacobs, the fourteen-year-old twins who Sam took care of, had recently joined the band as backup singers. Backup chanters. Well, something like that.

"Look how hot Becky looks!" Ian marveled.

"She's your girlfriend," Claudia reminded her son, a fond smile on her face.

Ah, young love. So uncomplicated, Carrie thought. Becky and Ian had recently become an item, and precocious Becky had been initiating Ian into the joys of kissing.

"So?" Ian protested. "She still looks hot."

"She looks great," Carrie said kindly. "And I'll probably use a picture of the band. But not that one. I want one that features the core members."

"How about this one, Carrie?" Claudia asked, holding up a photograph of a flooded wooden frame house that had a utility pole driven right through its roof.

"Wow," Carrie remarked, "I forgot about that one."

"You took it during the hurricane, right?" Claudia asked.

"Afterward," Carrie explained. "After the main blow, anyhow." Earlier in the summer, Hurricane Julius had barrelled up the east coast of the United States and slammed almost directly into Sunset Island. There had been widespread devastation. Carrie and her friends, along with Emma's former boyfriend, Kurt Ackerman, had been instrumental in rescuing residents from the poorer interior section of the island.

"I like that one," Carrie agreed. "Hold it aside."

"There's one of Dad!" Ian cried, grabbing another photo. It was one Carrie had taken at the big Graham Perry/Billy Joel concert out in San Francisco earlier that summer, when Carrie, Emma, and Sam all went out for the show. They also met Sam's birth mother, Susan Briarly.

"Put it aside," Carrie instructed him. "We'll start a pile of music shots."

"Hi!" a female voice called from the front hall. "It's me!"

Becky, Carrie thought. *Here to see Ian. I didn't know she was coming over.*

"We're in here!" Ian cried happily.

"Hi ya, Sam just dropped me off," Becky said from the kitchen doorway. "I told her I was invited." She was dressed in Daisy-Duke cut-off jeans and a short Sunset Island T-shirt that bared her midriff. Carrie noticed that Ian's eyes were nearly popping out of his head.

Carrie caught the look on Claudia's face—as if to say that Becky Jacobs looked entirely too grown-up for her son—but she didn't say a word about it.

"Hi, Becky," Claudia said, "want to help us?" She quickly explained to Becky what they all were doing.

"Not really," Becky answered honestly. She turned to Ian. "Want to go to your room and hang out?"

"I thought you were grounded," Claudia said sharply. "For the next week."

"Naw," Becky said smugly, "Dad changed his mind."

"Can I be excused, Mom?" Ian asked Claudia.

Carrie watched Claudia consider. "Okay," she said finally. "But leave your door open."

"Mom—" Ian protested.

"That's the deal. Take it or leave it," Claudia said cheerfully.

"Okay," Ian agreed, sighing dramatically. "Come on, Becky. We've got songs to work on, anyway."

"He's a handful," Claudia said cautiously, after he was gone.

"He's a good kid," Carrie commented, picking up another photo and examining it.

"It's her that I'm worried about," Claudia said dryly. "If you don't hear anything from up there, go check on them, okay?"

"Okay."

"But don't tell me what they're doing. I don't want to know!" Claudia laughed, taking a close look at a photo she'd picked out. It was another shot of Ian's band; in this one, Ian and Becky were holding hands, gazing rapturously into each other's eyes. She looked back over at Carrie. "Do you think I have to worry about them?"

"Worry how?" Carrie asked carefully.

Claudia considered for a moment. "Well, Becky is Ian's first girlfriend, but Becky seems . . . let's just say that she's probably a lot more experienced than Ian."

"Probably," Carrie agreed.

"I don't want Ian to get into anything he isn't ready for," Claudia explained.

"You mean . . . sex?" Carrie asked.

Claudia nodded. "God, he seems like such a baby to me! But I keep reading about kids having sex so young. And it's not like I'm not familiar with the whole sleazy world of rock and roll, groupies who are just scared, insecure, little girls—"

"I don't think you have to worry," Carrie interrupted softly.

"Carrie," Claudia sighed, reaching for another photo, "when it comes to sex, today everybody has to worry."

Even me, Carrie added to herself. *Even me.*

TWO

"Carrie, I'm itchy!"

"Wha-what?"

"I'm itchy!"

Carrie rubbed sleep out of her eyes. Her room was still dark, and she'd been fast asleep until Chloe's voice at her door had awakened her. She squinted at the luminous hands on the clock. It was 5:30 A.M.

I didn't know I was supposed to be on duty twenty-four hours a day, she thought, still half-asleep. *Where was I? Oh yes, Billy and I were on this fabulous yacht, with a whole crew to serve only us. We were sunbathing together on the bow as it sliced neatly through the warm waters of the Caribbean, sharing a big bowl of coconut and pineapple, then Billy leaned over and put his lips on mine, and—*

"Carrie, I'm really, really itchy!" Chloe cried, now standing at the foot of Carrie's bed.

Carrie's eyes popped open, and she sat up, now truly awake. "What is it, sweetie?"

"Everywhere itches on me," Chloe said in a little voice.

"Just a sec, honey," Carrie murmured to the little girl. She flipped on the small lamp on her nightstand.

"I'm itchy!" Chloe repeated for the fourth time, rubbing herself over and over.

"Here," she continued, pointing to her stomach. "And here," she said, pointing to her left thigh. "And here," she added, pointing to her shoulder.

"Anywhere else?" Carrie asked, sitting up in bed and looking at the small girl.

"Yup," Chloe replied. "Here and here and here and here." As she spoke, she pointed to various places on her body.

Carrie's first thought was that Chloe must have been attacked by a marauding band of bloodthirsty Maine mosquitoes as she slept. But Carrie was sure that when she put Chloe to bed she'd closed the bay windows in her room. And anyway, mosquitoes hadn't been much of a problem lately because the weather had been so dry.

What about poison ivy? Carrie thought. *No, she'd get that only on her hands and arms and legs. And she wasn't in the woods yesterday.*

"Lift up your nightshirt, sweetie," Carrie said in a soothing voice, while Chloe fidgeted uncomfortably and scratched.

"Okay," Chloe replied. She reached down, pulled the nightshirt over her head, and stood in her panties in front of Carrie.

Chloe was covered in little red bumps that looked like pimples just erupting. Some of the bumps were close together, while others were spread out.

Hmmm, Carrie thought. *Might be allergies, but I can't imagine to what. They don't look like bug bites. And definitely not poison ivy. Actually, it looks sort of like . . .*

A light went on in Carrie's mind. *That's it!* she thought. *It looks just like what my little brother had a couple of years ago. God, he was miserable.*

"Chloe?" Carrie asked.

"Yeah?

"Have you ever had the chicken pox?" Carrie queried.

"Chicken packs?" Chloe asked.

"No," Carrie corrected. "Chicken *pox*."

"No," Chloe said softly. "We don't even have a chicken!"

"You don't get it from a chicken," Carrie explained. "It's called that because . . . actually, I have no idea why it's called that."

"I don't want chicken packs," Chloe said, scratching her arm.

"Well," Carrie said, "I think you've got them sweetie."

"Will I die?" Chloe asked, a concerned tone in her voice.

"No," Carrie said, laughing reassuringly. "But you're going to itch for awhile. And you have to try not to scratch. I think we'd better go show your mom and dad."

"Did you ever have it?"

"Yup," Carrie answered. "It wasn't so bad." She got up and took her robe from behind the bathroom door.

"Mommy and Daddy are sleeping," Chloe pronounced. "And Daddy yells if you wake him up. Do we have to?"

"I think it's a good idea," Carrie replied. "They won't mind." *At least, I hope not,* she added to herself. "Come on."

"Okay," Chloe agreed, scratching her leg.

When they got to Graham and Claudia's suite, Carrie was surprised to see that the lights were already on and the door was open.

Ian was inside, standing near the bed. He was wearing nothing but a pair of pajama bottoms. And Claudia and Graham were peering closely at Ian's skin.

"Claudia?" Carrie said softly.

Claudia looked over at Carrie and

Chloe. "Hi," she said wearily. "I may be wrong, but I think Ian's got the chicken pox."

"Make that Ian and Chloe both have the chicken pox," Carrie replied with a tired smile.

"Is there such a thing as turkey pox?" Chloe asked in her small voice.

Graham laughed. "No darling," he said. "There is no such thing as the turkey pox. Or the pigeon pox. Come over here so I can look at you."

After checking out his daughter—she and Ian had identical red spots on their skin—Claudia suggested that he get the nail clippers from the medicine chest, a bottle of calamine lotion, and some cotton balls.

"What are the nail clippers for?" Graham asked as he walked to the bathroom.

"To cut their nails so they won't scratch," Claudia explained, taking the clippers and the lotion from Graham when he returned.

"Yeah, I guess that's obvious," Graham said, climbing back into bed. "Sorry, I was in the studio until about three hours ago. I'm still stupid from exhaustion."

Claudia kissed him on the head. "Go back to sleep, babe. We'll take care of the kids."

She and Carrie took Ian and Chloe into Chloe's room and clipped their nails, then they swabbed calamine lotion onto the red spots with cotton balls.

"Don't tell Becky," Ian said as his mother applied calamine lotion to the back of his legs. "I'll look like a total dork."

"Your secret is safe with me," Claudia said. As soon as the kids were covered with lotion, she told Ian to go get in bed and helped Chloe settle in.

"You want coffee?" Claudia asked Carrie as they walked out into the hall. "I don't think I'll be getting back to sleep now. Chicken pox!"

"I had it," Carrie noted.

"So did I," Claudia said. "My mom told me not to scratch. I think I ignored her."

"Me, too," Carrie said with a laugh.

"It's always something when you have kids," Claudia observed as the two of them walked downstairs.

"I'm in no hurry to find out," Carrie replied. "No hurry at all!"

"Chicken pox!" Billy laughed as he and Carrie sat together by the pool in the Templeton's backyard that afternoon. Billy had stopped by to say hello on his way to town to buy new strings for his guitar. He had a rotten cold and kept blowing his nose.

"I've already had my bout with chicken pox." Carrie grinned.

"Me, too." Billy smiled, sneezed, and wiped his nose again with a blue bandanna. "Right now I'd rather have that than this cold. God, it's miserable."

"Poor baby," Carrie commiserated, patting Billy gently on the shoulder.

"I've had it for days," Billy complained. "No one gets a cold in the summer!"

"Except you," Carrie said. "And please don't give it to me."

"Does that mean you're not going to nurse me back to health?" Billy teased her.

"That means Claudia took the kids to the doctor this morning for the official diagnosis, and she's counting on me to help out because Graham left for a tour this afternoon."

"Well, okay, but I bet you'll have more free time than usual," Billy pointed out. "And I plan to take advantage of that."

"Not unless you get wrapped in germ-proofing first," Carrie teased.

"Hey, I got this cold days ago, and I've already kissed you since then, so you've already got these killer germs," Billy playfully reminded her. He moved closer and fiddled with the top button on her shirt.

"I guess that's true," she agreed, unable to resist his touch.

"I knew you'd see it my way," Billy murmured. He leaned over and kissed her gently on the lips. "Want to go to the beach later?"

"How about you take care of the cold first and we go to the beach second?" Carrie suggested.

Billy sneezed and blew his nose again. "I'm so sick of this!" he said irritably. "This is my third cold since April!"

"You push yourself too hard," Carrie

observed, running her hand lovingly through his hair.

"No more than anyone else," Billy said, leaning back in his chaise lounge and soaking up some sun on his face. "Anyway, I'm sick of being sick."

The two of them were silent for awhile, now lying side by side on adjacent lounge chairs, their hands touching.

"Mmmm, that sun feels great," Billy said with a sigh. He turned his head to look at Carrie. "I've been thinking . . ."

"Uh-huh," Carrie murmured vaguely, feeling relaxed by the sun.

"No, this is a serious 'I've been thinking,'" Billy said.

Carrie opened her eyes and looked at him. "What?"

"About my taking the AIDS test," Billy said.

"So, what have you been thinking?"

"Can I tell you the truth?" Billy asked.

"Of course!" Carrie said. "Otherwise, what's the point?"

"I'm . . . I'm scared of taking it," Billy said after a moment's hesitation.

"It's just a blood test—"

"No," Billy said. "I'm not scared of the needle. I mean, what if I've got it? What if I'm positive? My whole life is over!"

A chill ran through Carrie's entire body. *Is Billy getting himself all worked up over nothing, or is there actually a chance that he slept with someone who he thinks might have AIDS? Or is he saying he shot drugs into his body with a needle? Or did he sleep around? Are there things about him I don't know?*

Carrie sat up and forced herself to speak calmly. "Why are you afraid?"

Billy didn't look at her. "I should think that was pretty obvious."

"No," Carrie replied. "It isn't. You've never used intravenous drugs, right?"

"Of course not," Billy answered. "I barely have a beer a month. I'm disgustingly clean-living."

"And you told me you've only slept with three girls in your life," Carrie recalled. "And that you used condoms with all three."

Billy wouldn't meet her gaze.

A chill came over Carrie again. *What if Billy isn't telling me the truth?*

"You told me the truth, didn't you?" she asked her boyfriend, looking very closely into his eyes.

Billy looked right back at her. "Yes . . . and no," he finally said.

Carrie's heart hammered in her chest. "What does that mean?"

"It means . . ." Billy began. "It means that once the condom broke."

Carrie was silent for a moment. "It broke?"

Billy nodded glumly.

"With who?" Carrie asked.

"What difference does it make?" Billy asked. "I don't want to discuss this with you!"

"Well, too bad," Carrie shot back, "because if you used a condom and it broke, that's just about as good as your not having used one at all!"

Silence hung in the air.

"Look, AIDS is hard to get," Carrie finally said, trying to control herself. "I read that. I mean, Arthur Ashe's wife hasn't gotten it.

"Do you happen to know if the girl you

slept with when the condom broke is sick?" Carrie asked in an even voice.

"I haven't seen her in a long time," Billy replied.

"And how long ago were you with her?" Carrie asked, hating the entire conversation.

"Two years ago," Billy admitted quietly.

"So . . ."

"That doesn't mean anything," Billy maintained. "I've done a lot of reading. The virus can stay in your body for ten years or more before you get sick."

"Did she ever get tested for HIV?" Carrie asked.

"I never asked."

This is the craziest thing, Carrie thought. *It's like I have to get a whole history of him before I can let myself sleep with him. It's like he's a witness on the stand and I'm the prosecutor!*

Carrie sighed. "I don't know what to say, Billy. Except . . . I think you should take the test—for both of us."

"There's something else I should tell

you," Billy continued grimly. "This girl . . . well, she was kind of wild."

Alarms went off in Carrie's head. "What does that mean?"

"It means . . . let's just say she and Diana De Witt would have a lot in common," Billy responded.

"Great," Carrie answered. "Just great." Both of them knew Diana's reputation for having reckless sex with a lot of guys. Neither of them knew whether Diana used protection, but it pretty much didn't matter in this case.

So Billy's slept with someone who slept with a lot of people. Great! Carrie thought. *That means that if I'm sleeping with him, I'm pretty much sleeping with everyone that girl ever slept with. Now that is disgusting.*

"Look, Billy," Carrie said, her voice tired, "I hate this."

"Me, too," Billy said.

"Why don't you just go get tested?" Carrie asked him. "I mean, if it's positive, it's positive. The test isn't going to change things."

"Except that I'll know," Billy said.

"Are you *really* worried?" Carrie asked him softly.

Billy nodded his head yes.

"Then just do it," Carrie advised him, touching his shoulder softly.

"If you do," Billy responded, looking at her.

Carrie was shocked. "What?"

"I said, I'll do it if you do," Billy repeated.

"Why should I?" Carrie asked quickly, before she had a chance to consider it. "You know the only person I've ever slept with was Josh. And we were both virgins at the time."

"How do I know you're telling me the truth?" Billy asked.

"Billy!" Carrie cried. "I can't believe you think I'd lie to you—"

Billy held up a hand to cut her off. "No, I know you didn't lie to me, Car," he assured her. "I'm not worried about you. I'm worried about Josh."

"But Josh—he told me that—"

"How do you know he was telling you the whole truth?" Billy asked. "How do you know he wasn't sleeping with someone else at the same time he was sleeping with you? Or that he hadn't screwed around before?"

"He wouldn't do that!" Carrie protested.

"Do you know for sure?" Billy asked. "I mean, really, truly, absolutely for sure?"

"No," Carrie admitted, "but—"

"I rest my case," Billy said, crossing his arms. He sneezed again and pulled out his bandanna to blow his nose. "Either we both go for the HIV test, or neither one of us goes."

THREE

That night, Sam made her way through the boisterous crowd at the Play Café and finally found Carrie sitting at their usual table under a video monitor. "You're not gonna believe this," she said when she got to the booth.

"Believe what?" Carrie asked. "That only you'd have the guts to wear that outfit?"

"I am *so* original," Sam crowed, twirling around so that Carrie could see her whole ensemble. She had on an antique navy-blue lace slip she'd found at a thrift shop, topped off with a jean jacket, and of course, her trademark red cowboy boots.

Carrie looked down at her own outfit—

baggy jeans, a T-shirt, and a flannel shirt—and sighed. "Do you think I blend into the crowd too much?" she asked Sam.

"Never," Sam said loyally. She slipped into the booth opposite Carrie. "Although, as you know, if I had your curves I'd show them off to their maximum potential." Sam craned her neck to look for the waitress. "Did you order yet?" she asked Carrie.

"No, I just got here," Carrie replied. "So what is it I won't believe?"

"I don't know how to break this to you," Sam said solemnly.

"Break *what?*" Carrie asked, a little worried that Sam had involved herself in yet another of her ongoing series of life crises. Sam had recently gone through some serious family problems—first, finding out she was adopted, then actually meeting her birth parents.

"It's about Becky," Sam said. "And Allie."

"Their father found cigarettes in their nightstand?" Carrie joked.

"Worse than that," Sam pronounced,

trying to catch the waitress's eye. "They have chicken pox. Hurrah! I'm free of them for a few days. Dan's hired a nurse."

A new waitress the girls didn't know hurried over to their booth. "Ya'll ready to order?" she asked them in a southern drawl.

"You're new," Sam said.

"Well, I started yesterday, and I already feel ancient," the waitress said with a tired grin. "I replaced Patsi—she took off with some guy."

"Patsi was our favorite waitress!" Sam exclaimed. "No offense," she added quickly.

"None taken," the pretty curly-haired blonde replied. "I'm Patsi's cousin, Marie. I live in Mississippi, and I was here visiting Patsi when she up and fell in love. So she's gone and I'm here!"

"That's lucky for you," Carrie commented. "Summer jobs on this island are hard to come by."

"Don't I know it," Marie agreed. "Well, Patsi ran off with Mr. Perfect, and I got to stay on the island, so I'd say we both got lucky! Anyway, are ya'll ready to order?"

Sam ordered a double order of nachos with everything, plus a pitcher of Coke, while Carrie rolled her eyes.

"Who's supposed to eat all that?" Carrie asked Sam.

"We'll invite cute, hungry guys over to help us graze, how's that?" Sam suggested. "So, pretty cool about the twins having chicken pox, huh?"

"It's an epidemic," Carrie said. "Ian's got 'em too. And Chloe. She woke me up at five thirty this morning to tell me."

"To tell you what?" a familiar female voice asked.

"Emma-bo-Bemma!" Sam cried, turning to say hello to her friend. "Join the table of the cutest girls in the place."

"You're biased," Emma said with a smile, sliding into the booth next to Sam.

"You look darling," Carrie told Emma. Emma was wearing white jeans and a sleeveless white lace T-shirt under a long embroidered white vest. She looked absolutely perfect, per usual.

"Here's what I want to know," Sam asked Emma. "How do you keep white clean all the time? I mean, I put some-

36

thing on, and it's dirty within five minutes. You live in white and dirt takes a walk."

"Oh, you know me," Emma teased Sam. "I'm so rich I never bother to wear anything more than once anyway."

"Hey!" Sam objected. "You can't make jokes about your money—that's my job!"

Emma laughed. "Beat you to it! Listen, you guys are never going to believe this!"

"All the Hewitt kids have chicken pox, right?" Sam said lightly, as if she'd seen it on the evening news.

"How did you know?!" Emma demanded.

Carrie cut in and explained about what had happened last night with the Templeton kids and with Becky and Allie Jacobs.

"They all go to the club together," Emma mused. "I guess it makes sense."

"Know what's really great?" Sam asked.

"What?" Emma replied.

"That just about every kid on this island who hasn't had 'em already is gonna get them!" Sam yelped.

"Why is that great?" Carrie asked.

"We'll have the island to ourselves,"

Sam predicted. "And there won't be any snotty kids around. For a week or so, I guess."

"Anyway," Emma said, "Jane took the kids to the doctor today."

"What did he say?" Carrie asked.

"He's a she," Emma answered, "and she said that they'll be fine in twelve days."

"I had them when I was eight," Carrie remembered.

"Ten," Sam said.

"Six," Emma said, grinning.

"Double nachos with everything," Marie said, placing a huge platter of food on the table. "And a pitcher of Coke. Enjoy!"

"Somehow this looks like a Sam order," Emma speculated.

"Only because I wasn't very hungry," Sam replied, reaching for a nacho. "So, what's up with you and Billy?" she asked Carrie, her mouth full.

"Gee, what a delicate segue," Emma said, daintily reaching for a small nacho.

"Ah, yes, Carrie and Billy," Sam intoned. "When we last left our intrepid heroine, she and her totally buff boyfriend—for whom she was panting with desire—had promised each other that they were going to talk about—"

"We did talk more about it," Carrie interrupted, pouring herself a glass of Coke.

"*Nu?*" Sam asked.

"*Nu?*" Carrie echoed. "What's '*nu*' mean?"

Sam grinned and licked some cheese off her finger. "It's an old Yiddish expression. My birth father taught it to me. It means, 'so?'"

"So, *nu?*" Emma asked, a shy smile on her face.

Sam and Carrie laughed, and Emma joined in. The idea of well-bred, Waspy Emma, whose ancestors probably came over on the Mayflower, using an expression that came from a language spoken by Eastern European Jews was just too hilarious for them to handle.

"We talked about it," Carrie said finally.

"And *nu?*" Sam asked again. "I really like that expression."

"Billy came over this afternoon and

we . . . had a discussion," Carrie explained, feeling very hesitant for some reason. *I don't want to tell them yet what Billy told me—about the condom breaking when he was with that girl,* Carrie thought to herself. *If I tell them, it will just make me more nervous about the whole thing! And maybe Billy wouldn't want me to tell anyone.*

"Girlfriend, cut to the chase, please," Sam ordered, reaching for another nacho. "Is he going for an AIDS test or not?"

"He is—" Carrie started to say. "He is."

"I guess you're glad about that," Emma said.

"It's not that simple," Carrie replied. "He'll only get one if I get one."

"Yeah, well, that makes sense," Sam said.

"It does?" Carrie asked.

"Yeah," Sam replied. "I can understand it."

"You can? Because I didn't—not at first, anyway," Carrie admitted.

"Well," Sam said seriously, "it makes sense. I mean, you're such a slut, you've

40

done it with everyone. It just goes to show—"

"Sam!" Emma cut her off. "This is serious." But even Carrie was laughing.

"Not that the test is really any good, anyway," Sam added, grabbing the last nacho.

"What do you mean?" Emma asked. "It's scientifically proven."

"Yeah," Sam responded, "but it only shows what got into your body six months ago or more."

"So you're saying if—" Emma spoke slowly, thinking through the implications of what Sam was saying.

"You got it," Sam interrupted. "Let's say, hypothetically, that Billy got an AIDS test tomorrow, and it was negative. That means that he didn't have the virus six months ago."

"But it doesn't tell what might have happened to him in the last six months, is that your point?" Emma asked.

"Yup," Sam said. "Isn't that wonderful news?"

"I think it's depressing!" Emma sighed.

"But Billy hasn't been with anyone

since we became a couple," Carrie pointed out. "And that's a lot more than six months ago."

"Maybe," Sam said, "but who can you trust? And how can you know for sure?"

"Well, if I can't trust him, I sure as hell better not be considering having sex with him!" Carrie exclaimed.

"Well, you can always get married, like . . ." Sam's voice trailed off, as she realized that she had brought up a subject that might better have been left alone. Emma and Kurt had almost gotten married; instead, they had split up forever. Kurt was so bereft he'd even left the island.

"It's okay, Sam," Emma said quietly. "It's okay to talk about it."

"Are you sure?" Carrie asked Emma, solicitous of her feelings. Carrie knew that Emma didn't much like to talk about Kurt—it was still just too painful for her.

Emma nodded and stirred the straw in her Coke. "I heard he's trying to get into the Air Force Academy in Colorado Springs."

"Well, that would be good," Carrie said softly. "Wouldn't it?"

Emma stared down at the table. "Who knows? When it comes to the subject of Kurt Ackerman, I don't really understand very much at all."

"Marriage wouldn't protect anyone from anything," Carrie said, leading them back to the topic at hand.

"Why not?" Sam asked.

"Because a lot of people have affairs, that's why," Carrie said slowly. "I read that like half of all married people have affairs."

"That is so gross." Sam snorted. "I mean, truly barf-city. Why get married if you can't be true? Who acts like that?"

"A lot of people," Emma said. "My mother for one."

Sam's eyebrows shot up. "Kat Cresswell of the perfect manners had an—"

"Well, I don't know for sure," Emma amended. "But I think she was already getting cozy with Austin Payne while my parents were still married."

"Gag me," Sam muttered. "At least that's something I never have to worry about with my parental units—the Kansas version, I mean. They barely kiss each other!"

"How about your birth mother?" Carrie reminded her. "When she and Michael made you, she and Carson were married, right?"

Sam took a sip of water before she answered. "Right" was her one-word response.

"So my point is," Carrie concluded, "that marriage doesn't guarantee anything."

"It should!" Emma cried.

"But it doesn't," Carrie said.

"It isn't fair," Emma cried passionately. "When I decide to make love, I want it to be perfect—the most beautiful, wonderful moment of my life."

"It should be," Carrie agreed.

"Not if you're so anxious you're going to die for doing it!" Emma cried.

"It *is* beautiful," Carrie said firmly. "If you really love each other, and you're committed to each other . . . I mean, it can be. It should be."

"So if you and Billy get tested, and

you're both negative," Sam asked, "are you still going to do it?"

"I think so," Carrie answered slowly.

"Well, you don't sound very psyched about it," Sam commented.

Carrie ran her finger over a crack in the table. "It doesn't seem very romantic anymore."

"Romance has gotten a lot of babes into a lot of trouble," Sam pronounced. "This is much better."

The girls all looked at each other. And none of them looked completely convinced.

FOUR

"So," the pleasant-looking woman in the white lab coat said to Carrie and Billy, "you both came here for an HIV test."

Carrie fidgeted as she sat in the doctor's office, nervously looking around at the walls. They were covered with official-looking diplomas and certificates. "Dr. Carol Mullins, M.D., Diplomat of the American Society of Family Practice Physicians," read one of them. There were many others. She looked over at Billy, and she could see that her boyfriend was pretty fidgety, too.

The two of them had talked the morning after their conversation in the

Templetons' backyard, and they'd simply decided to waste no more time but just go for their tests together. They decided they'd get the tests done by the same local physician who was treating Ian and Chloe's chicken pox.

"Even if we get the test, we can always decide not to get the results," Carrie had told Billy.

"Yeah, right," Billy had replied sarcastically. He reached for a tissue. "Damn this cold, anyway."

Carrie had smiled weakly. "Dumb suggestion," she agreed. "I'm just nervous."

"Me, too," Billy agreed, and he'd given Carrie a small hug.

But they had called Dr. Mullins, and made a couple of appointments for a week later, which was as soon as the doctor could fit them in. Then, the very same day Dr. Mullins' office had called and said there was a cancellation—could Carrie and Billy come in together? Both of them were free that afternoon, and both went.

"I can't believe I'm actually doing this," Carrie said to Billy in the waiting room, where the two of them had spent a half-hour with three more kids who looked like they had the chicken pox, before they were finally ushered into Dr. Mullins's office.

"I can't believe it either," Billy had remarked.

"How do you feel?" Carrie asked him.

"Like there's a noose around my neck."

"Why?"

"I can't say," Billy had mumbled. "I just can't say."

Now, they were actually sitting in the office together, and Dr. Mullins was giving them her standard pretest counseling. She had explained that the test was not actually for the disease, but for antibodies to the virus that most scientists believed caused the disease, called the human immunodeficiency virus, or HIV.

She asked, in a very frank voice, for Carrie and Billie to tell her their sexual histories. They did—and they were the same stories they had told each other a few days before.

"I must say," Dr. Mullins said, when they had finished talking, "that the two of you are both at very low risk for having contracted AIDS. You've had very few partners, you've practiced safer sex, you're not intravenous drug users or partners of intravenous drug users, and neither of you has hemophilia."

"As far as I know," Billy said, managing to smile.

"You'd know," Dr. Mullins answered. "Believe me, you'd know."

The best thing about her is that she's so frank and direct, Carrie thought. *She's not judging us for being here. She didn't even ask if we were getting married.*

Dr. Mullins then gave them a mini-lecture about "safer" sex. "We call it safer sex as opposed to safe sex for a reason," Dr. Mullins explained. "The only totally safe sex is with one's self, or to abstain completely."

Carrie and Billy nodded.

"It's just an important point to keep in mind," the doctor said mildly. "Condoms are crucial, if one decides to have a sexual relationship, but they are not fool-proof. They can break."

Carrie snuck a quick look at Billy, who

looked even more uncomfortable than before.

"It's also important to use latex condoms," the doctor continued in her matter-of-fact voice. "And the woman should use a spermicidal foam or jelly, for additional protection against AIDS and other sexually transmitted diseases."

Carrie gulped hard. *What I really want to do is to just run out of here and forget about the whole thing,* she thought. *I hate this!*

"Let me explain one other thing," Dr. Mullins said, "before I see you individually. The tests are totally confidential."

"That's what they say," Billy responded. "But I never understood how."

"Most blood tests go to a private lab," Dr. Mullins explained. "But all our AIDS tests go to a state lab. And your tests will go in by number, not by your name. That's the law."

"So no one will know the results except us?" Carrie asked.

"That's right," Dr. Mullins replied.

"Yeah," Billy said skeptically, "well, I read that once—"

Dr. Mullins cut him off. "That was before they instituted laws about using numbers. My patients' confidentiality does not get breached. Period. End of discussion. Okay?"

Carrie looked over at Billy. Nervous perspiration dotted his forehead. "You don't have to do this if you don't want to," Carrie said to him softly.

"I'm doing it," Billy said, gritting his teeth. Carrie actually saw a bead of perspiration slide down his temple past his left ear. He brushed it away quickly.

He's really upset, she thought to herself anxiously. *What if there's something he's hiding from me?*

"Okay?" Dr. Mullins asked. "Are there any questions?"

"This might be a dumb question," Billy began, "but I have a chest cold. Will this affect my blood test?"

"No," the doctor replied. "Anything else?"

Carrie and Billy both shook their heads no.

"I'll see Carrie first, then," the doctor said.

Carrie swallowed hard and followed Dr. Mullins into an examining room. Billy went out and sat in the waiting room again.

Carrie only spent a couple of minutes with the doctor. A nurse drew some blood and handed her a form to sign which said that she agreed to be tested for HIV, and that was that. Billy, when he got called in, spent a lot longer. So long, in fact, that Carrie had gotten worried while waiting for him in the reception area.

"What happened?" she asked him as he came out.

"I told her about all the colds I've been getting," Billy said. "And that I just haven't been feeling all that well."

"So?"

"So she gave me a full exam," Billy explained, "and took a few blood samples."

"That's probably a good idea," Carrie ventured.

"I don't want to get the chicken pox," Billy tried to joke. Then he saw the concerned look on Carrie's face. "Don't worry. Remember, I've already had them."

Okay, Carrie thought, *now's the time to*

ask him about why he was so nervous about the AIDS test. It's now or never.

She asked, and Billy got even more uncomfortable looking.

"Look," he replied, "I said I couldn't talk about it."

"About what?" Carrie prodded.

"About it!" Billy yelled. Two young girls who had been scratching their arms stopped to look at him. He pulled Carrie into a corner of the waiting room. "I'm sorry," he told her. "I'm just tense."

"What's wrong?" Carrie asked him. "I've never seen you like this!"

Billy sighed. "Look," he said in a low voice, "we're having a band meeting tomorrow at noontime. I haven't even told Sam and Emma yet, but why don't you come along?"

"What does the band have to do with anything?" Carrie asked with frustration.

"Everything," Billy intoned. "Everything."

Billy, Presley Travis—the bass player and Sam's former boyfriend—and Jay

Bailey, who played keyboards, were sitting together in the large, run-down living room of the house they rented when the girls arrived. The only member of the band who was missing was Sly Smith, the drummer, who had recently gone home to Baltimore, Maryland, after contracting a bad case of pneumonia.

Sly had been temporarily replaced as drummer by Nick Trenton, a rangy surfer whom Sam had developed an immediate crush on. But as Carrie, Sam, and Emma sat together—Diana De Witt, per usual, was sitting on the other side of the room, looking supercilious—Carrie could see that Nick was nowhere to be found.

"Okay, let's get started," Billy said, resettling himself on the couch. Billy looked distinctly uncomfortable, and Carrie still couldn't figure out why.

"What's Carrie doing here?" Diana asked sharply from her perch near Pres. "Last time I checked, she wasn't part of this group."

"She's here because I asked her to be here," Billy responded, just as sharply. "Do you have a problem with that?"

"Well, it's just . . . anyway, where's Nick?" Diana asked.

"He's out of the band," Billy said simply.

"Ooo, Sammi's going to be sooo depressed," Diana cooed. "As for me, I've had the pleasure of . . . oh, never mind. That was the only good thing about him."

Billy ignored her crack. "We found out he stole some equipment during a gig we did in Portland," Billy said. "He's out. And we're better off without him."

"But who's going to drum?" Sam asked.

"Sly!" Billy called, a bit of a quaver in his voice.

Sly? Carrie thought. *But I thought that Sly was still in the hospital. . . .*

Sly Smith walked into the room. Carrie, Sam, and Emma let out a collective gasp of surprise.

Oh, my God, he's so much thinner, Carrie thought to herself. *He was slender to begin with, but now he looks like he's lost maybe twenty pounds. He looks like he hasn't eaten in a month! He must have been really, really sick.*

"I'm back," Sly said wanly.

Then all the members of the band, even Diana, burst into applause. The girls all ran over and hugged Sly. Tears came to Sly's eyes. He brushed them away with the back of his hand.

Sly sat down on the couch next to Billy and Pres, and everyone else settled happily back down.

"We're so glad you're back!" Emma cried.

Everyone began firing questions at the drummer, and Billy finally called for quiet.

"I think Sly has something he wants to say," Billy said in a tight voice.

Everyone looked expectantly at Sly. He had always been very outspoken and opinionated—Carrie remembered that, when the band had added backup singers to their mix, Sly had been the band member most adamantly opposed to the decision. Still, everyone respected him for his professionalism and drumming abilities.

"So, what's up?" Diana asked casually.

"You leaving us for Guns n' Roses or something?"

"Not quite," Sly replied in a shaky voice. His eyes scanned the room, and he took a deep breath. "What I needed to tell you all is . . . I have AIDS."

Everyone in the room seemed to hold their breath.

"I have AIDS," Sly repeated more firmly, gulping hard. "I've been in the hospital because I got Pneumocystis carinii pneumonia, which is an infection of the lungs that a lot of people with AIDS get. I'm better now. The pneumonia is gone."

No one said anything. Carrie looked at her friends Emma and Sam, and they were both as white as a sheet. Sam, in fact, was trembling. Carrie looked down at her own hands. They were trembling, too.

I just hugged Sly, Carrie thought anxiously. *I just hugged someone with AIDS. But that's crazy. You can't get AIDS from hugging someone with AIDS. Can you? How long has Billy known this? No wonder he was so freaked out about getting tested.*

"I'm better now," Sly continued, his voice low. "And I'm planning to be the Flirts' drummer for a long time to come."

Diana raised her eyebrows, but she didn't say anything.

"Just because I have AIDS doesn't mean that I'm a cripple," Sly said earnestly, "or that I have to stay in bed all the time, or that I'm going to die tomorrow. Because I'm not planning to die anytime soon."

Pres reached over and touched Sly's arm, and Sly smiled at him. Then he turned back to the group.

"Now, I'm probably the first person you've ever met who has AIDS," Sly said. "Hell, *I'm* the first person I ever met who I *knew* had AIDS—"

"Then how did you get it?" Diana asked him.

Sly gazed at her. "That's irrelevant, don't you think?"

Diana shrugged uncomfortably.

"I have theories about how I might have gotten the virus," Sly said. "But I don't know for sure. That's not what I want to talk about, anyway. I want to tell you that what they say on TV is absolutely true. You can't get it from touching me. You can't get it from hugging me. You can't get it from me sneezing on you."

Carrie glanced over at Emma and Sam again. She saw tears in Emma's eyes. And Sam had turned even more white, if that was possible.

"Are you gay?" Diana blurted out.

Sly shook his head at her in obvious disgust. "Diana, wake up and smell the coffee. This isn't a gay disease. Anyone can get it. Anyone. Even you."

Diana turned even whiter than Sam, and she looked away from Sly.

"I hope you can accept what I'm saying," Sly continued earnestly. "Maybe you can't. That doesn't matter either, except that we'll be a better band if you can. That's all I have to say."

Tears spilled over from Carrie's eyes, and she watched as Billy reached over and hugged Sly, holding him tight.

"Oh, yeah, one last thing," Sly said, when Billy pulled away. "Billy, Pres, and Jay have known since I got admitted to the hospital. I asked them not to tell you guys. I wanted to be able to tell you myself." He turned to look at Billy, a look of love and admiration on his face. "I see that they kept their word."

FIVE

The entire band watched in silence as Sly left the room. In fact, no one said anything until they heard the back screen door slam.

"Where did he go?" Emma asked softly.

"To hang out in the backyard, I think," Pres replied. "He's giving us time to discuss this."

"Sly wants us to decide whether he should stay in the band or not," Billy explained. Carrie noticed that the color had returned to Billy's face and he was beginning to speak with some of his usual authority.

"What are you talking about?" Sam asked, pushing some hair back from her face. "He's back, he's in the band, that's that. What's the biggie?"

"Over my dead body," Diana seethed.

"Now, that I could arrange," Sam replied sweetly.

For once Diana ignored her. "He can't be in. What are we doing here—committing group suicide? I mean—"

"Hey, hold on, Diana," Billy cut in. "That is a ridiculous statement."

"Ridiculous, my butt!" Diana exclaimed self-righteously. "I value my life, even if you don't."

"See, this is just what Sly told me he thought would happen," Billy stated, sounding exhausted. He reached for a tissue and blew his nose. "So he told me that he wanted a unanimous decision that he's in. Otherwise, he's taking himself out."

"Otherwise," Pres clarified in his easy Tennessee drawl, "he's just gonna head on home to Maryland. No hard feelin's, he says. But I, for one, don't want to see that happen."

Wow, Carrie thought. *Sly left the room because he wanted to give everyone a chance to speak openly. He wants people to say what's really on their minds. I never knew he had so much character.*

"So, let me understand this," Diana said. "Do I get to vote? Or is this another one of those the-backup-singers-don't-count kind of deals?"

"Yeah, you get to vote," Billy informed her. "We're changing the rules just this once."

"What about your girlfriend?" Diana asked, looking Carrie over coolly. "What's she doing here? I thought this was *band* business."

"She's here because I value her opinion," Billy said, reaching for one of the cans of soda he'd brought out earlier and placed on the table. He cracked the soda open and took a big swig. "And you should, too."

"Whatever," Diana mumbled. "So long as she doesn't vote."

"I don't think of it as a vote," Billy answered, clearly trying not to lose his temper at Diana. "We've got to reach a unanimous consensus."

"What's that?" Sam asked, and Carrie

realized that it was only the second time that her usually irrepressible friend had opened her mouth since Sly's announcement.

She must really be upset by it, Carrie thought, *and as usual she's hiding it. Well, I can't say I blame her.*

"It means we've all got to agree," Pres said gently. "If'n we don't all agree, it's as if we all are tellin' him no. That's the way he sees it, and that's the way he wants it."

"So," Billy summed up, "the floor is open."

"Let's vote," Diana said quickly. "There's nothing to discuss."

No one seemed to have a better idea, so Billy leaned forward and reached for some slips of paper on the coffee table.

"What are those for?" Emma asked.

"Sly wants it secret," Billy explained. "He doesn't want anyone saying he should be in the band because it's politically correct or something."

Wow, Carrie thought. *This is a different Sly from the guy who left here to go to Maryland. He's a lot more thoughtful.*

And then another voice spoke inside her head: *Maybe you get a lot more thoughtful when you know you're going to die a horrible, ugly death.* A cold shiver crawled up her spine.

Billy tore the paper into seven pieces, and tossed them to everyone. "Just write 'yes' or 'no' on it, fold it up, and toss it in this baseball cap," he ordered, holding out a Boston Red Sox cap upside down. Pres passed a few pencils around, and Carrie watched everyone write down their choice and put it in the cap. When they were done, Billy took the cap back and started opening slips of paper.

A frown crossed his face.

"It's not unanimous," he announced.

"Who voted no?" Sam demanded, looking at Diana pointedly.

"It doesn't matter," Billy answered, dropping all the slips of paper back into the hat. "I don't know and I really don't care." He looked around at the group. "And anyway, it was more than one person."

The silence in the room felt thick to

Carrie, as if it were harder to breathe. The temperature seemed to rise.

"Well, I'm not a chicken," Diana finally said. "I'll take credit. I voted no."

"How could you?" Sam demanded. "Never mind, I know how you could—"

"Sam, shut up," Diana snapped. "It's not that I have anything against Sly, or against anyone with AIDS, for that matter. . . ."

"Then what?" Sam demanded again.

"It's just that it wouldn't be good for the band," Diana said, sounding uncomfortable. "It's purely a professional thing."

"I hate to say it," Jay said, clearing his throat, "but . . . uh . . . I can understand her point of view."

Billy looked at Jay hard, and Jay flushed. "You?" Billy asked softly.

"Look, Sly is my friend," Jay said defensively. "This isn't about that—"

"How can you agree with Diana?" Sam blurted out, staring hard at Jay. "Sly's not contagious. It isn't like he's a . . . a murderer or something!"

"I'm not saying that I agree with her,"

Jay said evenly. "I'm just saying I understand her point of view."

"So do I," Billy spoke up.

Billy, what are you saying? Carrie thought, aghast.

"I'm not saying I agree," he added quickly, "but I think a lot of you will listen if I say it instead of Diana."

"That's for sure," Sam muttered, folding her arms warily.

"What Diana's thinking is that if Sly stays in the band, everything is going to be about Sly having AIDS, instead of the music the Flirts are making," Billy said evenly. "Have I summed it up correctly, Diana?"

Diana nodded. "That's exactly my point."

"Oh, yeah, right," Sam snorted. "A minute ago you were saying all this crap about how you value your life—"

"Well, now I'm talking about something else," Diana insisted. "If Sly stays in the band, we might as well change our name to Flirting With AIDS, because that's how everyone is going to think of us."

"That isn't funny," Pres remarked.

Diana shrugged. "Anyway, I don't think it's good for the band for all the attention to be about Sly and his disease."

Emma spoke up for the first time. "Don't you think it will be good for people out there to see that you can have AIDS and still be productive?" she asked softly.

"Maybe," Diana allowed, "but it's too iffy. *If* he's not sick. *If* he doesn't get sick. *If* people don't stay away from our shows because they're afraid *they'll* get sick."

"You can't get AIDS that way," Billy reminded her. "Everyone knows that."

"You think so?" Diana asked. "One day I read that the virus is in saliva, and the next day I read that maybe it's in tears, but you probably won't get AIDS from either. How do we know what they'll find out tomorrow?"

"That's ridiculous!" Emma affirmed.

"People aren't going to think they're being ridiculous," Diana maintained. "Just careful."

"What, you think people are going to stay away from our gigs because they thinks AIDS can, like, *attack* them through the air?" Sam asked Diana sarcastically.

"You know, if you had a half a brain, I might bother to respond to that," Diana tossed off.

"What do you think, Carrie?" Billy asked, turning to her. "Since you're not in the band, you're the only one here with an objective opinion."

Carrie took a long time before she answered Billy's question.

"I think," she began, "that you're all assuming too much."

"What do you mean?" Billy asked her.

"There's no way to know how people are going to react to Sly being in the band until they actually do," Carrie explained slowly.

"That's true," Pres agreed.

"And there's no way to know how sick he's going to be unless he gets sick," Carrie continued. "And he says he's doing better, now." She could see Emma and Sam both nodding, and it encouraged her.

"And lastly," Carrie added, "Sly always had the best interests of the band in mind. If it looks like it's not working out, he'll quit."

"That's good," Diana said, "because we sure couldn't fire him. How would that look?"

"He'd quit," Billy said firmly, backing up Carrie. "Anyway, I think Carrie's right."

"Not only is Carrie right," Pres said, "but there's this little thing about friendship and loyalty—remember that? Sly is a member of this band. An important member. And he's my friend. I do not turn my back on a friend."

Billy nodded and turned to Jay. "Jay?"

"I thought this was supposed to be anonymous," Jay reminded Billy.

Billy shrugged. "It's too late for that now."

Jay took a deep breath. "Well, I can still see Diana's point," he said slowly. "But I'm willing to give it a try." He looked over at Pres. "He's my friend, too."

"Sam?" Billy asked.

"In," Sam replied.

"Emma?"

"I agree with Sam."

"Diana?" Billy asked, as everyone turned to look at her.

Diana cocked her head to one side. "I'm being railroaded."

No one said a word.

"Okay, okay," she finally agreed. "Because he's a good drummer, he stays for now. But if things change, we have to vote again."

"Okay," Billy said with a smile of relief, "Sly's in. I'll go tell him."

"So now I hope you understand why I was so upset," Billy said to Carrie, as the two of them sat on one of the benches out at the end of the pier off the main beach. Because rain was forecast, there was almost no one around, except for a couple of men working crab traps halfway down the pier. It was after dinner that night, and Claudia had given Carrie the evening off when it became clear that there really wasn't very much work for her to do, since both Ian and Chloe were in bed.

"I do," Carrie agreed, reaching for Billy's hand. "I still can't believe he has

AIDS." She looked up at the darkening sky.

"Believe it," Billy answered. "Although I couldn't believe it at first, either."

"It sure doesn't make the chicken pox seem very important," Carrie remarked, nuzzling her head against Billy's shoulder.

"That's for sure," Billy answered. The two of them sat silently for a time.

"Can I ask you a question?" Carrie asked, finally.

"Sure," Billy answered, putting his arm around her protectively. A few drops of rain began to fall, spattering against the rough wood of the pier. Carrie opened the umbrella she'd brought with her, and Billy held it over them.

"What would you do if I got sick?" Carrie asked. "I mean, really sick."

"Like AIDS sick?" Billy asked.

"Okay, like AIDS sick."

"I don't know," Billy said honestly. "It's so weird, because I've been asking myself the same question."

"You've been asking yourself what

you'd do if my test comes back positive?" Carrie asked with surprise.

"Not that specifically," Billy qualified, watching the raindrops fall around them. "But, let's say—oh, cancer, or lupus, or multiple sclerosis—"

Carrie shivered. "This is the most depressing conversation I've ever had."

Billy's arm tightened around her. "It would be a lot more depressing if you actually had any of those things." He gently reached up and pushed a lock of hair off of Carrie's face. "I guess I'd take care of you," Billy said slowly. He leaned over and gave her a soft kiss.

"And I'd take care of you," Carrie replied. "But how can you live knowing you're going to die—"

"I don't think Sly looks at it that way."

"Maybe not," Carrie said. "But unless a miracle cure comes along, it's true. What if you love someone, and they get AIDS? What if it means giving up your life?"

Billy stared at her, troubled.

"I saw a documentary once about someone dying of AIDS," Carrie began. "It took a really long time, and the man was really,

really sick at the end—the virus invaded the guy's brain and his lover's entire life was just caring for this person that he loved. . . ."

Carrie couldn't finish. She felt tears come to her eyes. It was just too horrible for her to consider, this idea of getting really sick and dying.

"Car, I love you," Billy said slowly. "If you needed me . . . I'd be there."

"Right back atcha," Carrie said, using a Sam expression to try to lighten the mood. She gave a ragged laugh. "Gee, this is a fun conversation."

Billy sneezed. "This rain might not be the best thing for my cold," he considered, pulling out his freshly washed bandanna and blowing his nose.

"Come on," Carrie said, pulling Billy up by his hands. She wrapped her arms around him and he held the umbrella over them. "Nothing is going to happen to us," she told him fervently. "We're young. And healthy. We can concentrate on having fun." She stood on tiptoe to kiss him.

"I bet that's what Sly thought," Billy

answered, not able to let go of their somber conversation.

"Do you know how he got it?" Carrie asked.

"Does it matter?" Billy responded.

"No, but . . . well, I'm curious."

"Sly doesn't know," Billy answered. "Or if he does know, he's not telling."

"Have you had a chance to talk with him about this?" Carrie queried. "I mean, about how he feels about it?"

"I tried." Billy sighed. "Pres tried. But we got nowhere. Sly seemed to be treating it like he has the chicken pox."

"Psych 101—it's called denial," Carrie said. "Meaning when you can't deal with something really horrible, you pretend it isn't happening or it isn't so bad."

"Yeah, I follow," Billy replied.

"Well, can you blame him?"

"What do you mean?"

"What's he supposed to do, sit around all day and think about how he's going to die?" Carrie remarked.

Billy was silent again. "Gee, I'm in a great mood," he said finally.

Hand in hand, they headed back toward the car, both of them lost in thought.

"We get our tests back soon," Carrie finally said when they got back to the car.

Billy didn't say a word. He just unlocked the car doors and got in.

Carrie got in, too, and slammed the door. The rain grew harder, pelting down onto the windshield.

Here I am, alone with Billy, the entire night off, and sex is absolutely the last thing on my mind, she realized morosely. *What I really want is to go back to being a little kid, before I had to worry or even think about any such thing as AIDS.*

SIX

"Carrie! You came!" Emma exclaimed with surprise when she saw her friend later that evening.

"Yeah," Carrie agreed laconically, sliding into a seat around the small cocktail table where Sam and Emma were already sitting. Emma had called her earlier and asked if she wanted to go with her and Sam to hear a reggae-jazz quartet play at the cocktail lounge of the Sunset Inn. Carrie had declined, since she had expected to spend the whole evening with Billy. But when Billy had driven her home, he'd felt so miserable from his cold, and they were both so depressed, that they decided to call it a night. Carrie had still felt antsy, and so she'd decided to go join her friends after all.

"Did you and Billy have a fight?" Sam asked her.

"No, not really," Carrie replied with a deep sigh.

"Are you okay?" Emma asked solicitously. "You look awful."

"I'm okay," Carrie said listlessly. She looked over at her two friends and noticed they were dressed up. Emma had on white linen shorts with a matching white linen vest, and Sam had on sheer diaphanous black pants with a sleeveless black leotard that featured mesh from the neck to the cleavage. Looking around the room, Carrie noted that everyone else was dressed up, too. "I guess I should have changed," she added, looking down at the outfit of jeans and a red cotton sweater she'd worn for her walk on the beach with Billy.

"It's not important," Emma assured her.

"We're just glad you're here," Sam added warmly.

Carrie grinned. *I have the world's two greatest friends. They care about me so much!*

"So," Sam continued in her usual brazen fashion, "why do you feel like dogmeat?"

"Would you care to order?" a waiter asked Carrie formally.

"An iced tea, please," Carrie said, and the waiter walked away. She looked around the room again. It was packed with well-dressed, happy, wealthy people. People who could afford to live on Sunset Island. Healthy people. People who didn't have AIDS.

"How's the band?" Carrie asked, trying to put her mind on something else.

"They're great," Emma said enthusiastically. "Very unique. They call themselves A Hot Ganja Minute."

"Ganja as in marijuana?" Carrie asked with surprise.

Sam laughed. "Yeah, they're Rastifarians, so smoking pot is part of their religion or something. Anyway, they combine reggae and jazz—it's very terrif."

Emma leaned forward conspiratorially, a twinkle in her eye. "Personally, I don't think anyone informed the Sunset Inn entertainment committee what 'ganja' means, or these guys would never have gotten booked!"

They all laughed.

"If Kristy Powell gets ahold of this one for the *Breakers*, it'll be big news!" Sam crowed.

Emma cocked her head toward the other side of the room. "She's here, sitting with a gorgeous guy over in the corner."

Sam craned her head around. "Hey, do you think that's the mysterious fiancé we heard about?"

"Can you imagine Kristy Powell married?" Emma wondered. "That's almost as bizarre as imagining Diana De Witt married!"

"Or Lorell!" Sam agreed.

Silence fell across the table. The waiter set down Carrie's iced tea and strode away.

More silence.

"We're not doing a very good job at

pretending there's nothing important on our minds, are we?" Emma finally admitted.

Carrie shook her head no and sipped her tea. "I just . . . I feel like crying every five minutes. The whole thing is so depressing. Sly's going to die."

"Maybe there'll be some more new drugs soon," Emma suggested.

"Maybe," Carrie said, not sounding very convinced. "But if you get Pneumocystis carinii pneumonia, you're already pretty sick."

"Gruesome." Sam shuddered.

"How do you live," Carrie mused, "knowing that you're going to die?"

"Everyone's going to die," Emma pointed out.

"Yeah," Carrie allowed. "But we don't think about it. We don't live with it every day. We're young! We're not supposed to have to!"

Sam twirled the cocktail straw in her cranberry juice. "I wonder what would happen," Sam's voice got a little wistful, "if I got really sick?"

"Sam, you're fine—" Emma protested.

"I know," Sam agreed. "But, I mean, what if I wasn't fine? What would happen to me?"

"You'd have two of the best nurses in the world to take care of you—right Emma?" Carrie said instantly.

"Right!" Emma said. "There's nothing I wouldn't do for you."

Carrie smiled shakily at her friends.

"Are you okay?" Emma asked, a look of real concern on her face.

"Sure, I'm fine," Carrie said in a monotone.

"Then why are you the color of a hospital sheet?" Sam demanded.

"I am?" Carrie replied, dodging uncharacteristically.

"Is it something about Billy?" Emma asked cautiously.

Carrie took a sip of iced tea. Her hands were trembling and she put them in her lap. "Look, it's silly. I know I'm overreacting. But . . . Billy told me something that really freaked me out." She told her friends the story Billy had told her about

84

his condom breaking when he'd been with his old girlfriend.

"Whoa," Sam breathed, her eyes wide. "It just . . . broke?"

Carrie nodded miserably. "And this girl was evidently promiscuous. He compared her to Diana."

"Oh, Car," Emma commiserated, touching her friend's arm in sympathy.

"And I feel . . . livid!" Carrie realized. "That's how I feel! I'm angry that he ever had sex with anyone—I know that's not reasonable, but it's how I feel! And I'm angry that he had sex with a girl who slept around, too. What could he have been thinking? And I'm *really* angry that his condom broke and now all this past stuff has to be a part of *my* life!" She looked miserably at her friends. "God, what if his AIDS test comes back positive? What will I do?"

No one said a word for a long moment.

"You love Billy, right?" Emma finally asked.

"I do," Carrie confirmed. "With all my heart."

"Then you'll just have to take it as it

comes, I guess," Emma said. "I mean, I suppose that sounds like lame advice—"

"Look, does Billy know that this girl was HIV positive?" Sam broke in.

Carrie shook her head no.

"Well, then, you're probably getting yourself all bent out of shape over nothing," Sam concluded. "What did that president once say—something about fearing fear?"

"It was Franklin Roosevelt," Carrie explained. "'The only thing we have to fear is fear itself.'"

"Yeah, right," Sam agreed. "I heard that in American history class in high school, but I was busy sketching cute outfits in my notebook."

"Figures," Carrie said with a laugh that helped break the tension.

"Sam's probably right, you know," Emma agreed softly. "You probably don't have a thing to worry about."

Carrie smiled ruefully. "Somehow when it comes to this, 'probably' just doesn't seem definite enough."

A Hot Ganja Minute returned to the small stage and launched into a reggae version of the jazz classic "Take the A Train." Carrie tried to lose herself in the music, but scary questions kept chasing around and around in her head.

What if Billy actually has AIDS? What would I really do? Not what would I want myself to do, but what would I really do?

"Ladies and gentlemen—" an amplified voice boomed out over the sound system "—please welcome back to the stage of the Play Café, Sunset Island's very own Flirting With Danger!"

Word of the Flirts' impromptu show had made its way around the island like wildfire, and one of the local radio stations had actually broadcast several announcements about the show—one of their DJs said that the Flirts were his favorite local band—so the Play Café was absolutely packed.

At Billy's request, a table had been set up at the door, requesting a five-dollar donation from everyone who came in, with the money to be donated to Maine CARES, an AIDS service organization active in the state. Everyone seemed delighted to give, and just before the band went on, a club employee came backstage to say that nearly a thousand dollars had been collected.

Carrie, who had been hanging out backstage with the band, squeezed her way into the front of the crowd by the stage. She was determined to take her best concert photos ever—maybe even some that she would include in her portfolio for the Yale project.

It took a moment before the band came charging onto the stage in their customary fashion, and a chant went up from several people in the impatient crowd.

"F-L-I-R-T-S, Flirts, Flirts, Flirts!"

The whole crowd then picked it up, and the chant became deafening.

Then the band hit the stage. A sustained cheer rang out when Sly climbed behind his drumset and let fly with a tremendous drumroll. Most of the crowd had heard rumors by now that he had AIDS.

As Sly was hitting his snare drum, Emma, Sam, and Diana ran out. The crowd cheered, whooped, and whistled. They were wearing their all-white fringed, sleeveless nylon minidresses with round necklines, and matching white patent leather go-go boots. The band had bought them these outfits for the big East Coast tour, and the girls looked great.

Finally, as the crowd noise reached its peak, Billy launched into their opening number, "Love Junkie."

> You want too much
> And you want it too fast
> You don't know nothin'
> About makin' love last
> You're a love tornado
> That's how you get your kicks
> You use me up
> And move on to your next fix.
> You're just a Love Junkie
> A Love Junkie, baby,
> A Love Junkie
> You're drivin' me crazy . . .

The crowd went completely crazy on the chorus. All around Carrie, people were yelling out the lyric "love junkie!", stabbing the air with their fists, dancing and boogying with abandon.

When the song ended, whoops, hollers, and applause filled the café. A chant of "Sly! Sly! Sly!" went up, and Sly stood up behind his drums and nodded his head in acknowledgment. Carrie caught a photo of him at just that moment, his thin face a mixture of emotions. Billy tried to say a few words, but the crowd was too excited to listen. So he smiled his usual wry grin, and Carrie snapped a shot. Billy shrugged boyishly, turned to the band, and they moved right into "Wild Child," which featured Sam, Diana, and Emma in a hot dance number.

I'd say, Carrie thought to herself happily, as the crowd got more and more pumped up, *that this is going pretty well. And I'd also say*—Carrie took a quick glance at Sly, who hadn't missed a beat all night—*the one big question about the band and the people on this island has been answered.*

She looked over at Pres and remembered what he'd said: you don't turn your back on a friend.

"Wow," Sly said as he thirstily guzzled a Coke backstage in the Play Café's dressing room after the show. "Double-wow."

"You were great, my man," Pres said as he pulled off the perspiration-soaked T-shirt he was wearing and replaced it with a dry one.

Carrie hovered around, snapping even more pictures.

Billy stuck his tongue out at Carrie's camera, then he grinned. "You look awfully fine behind that camera, babe," he told her.

"Tell me again. I want to catch that exact look on your face," Carrie said, snapping more shots.

"How about if I show you?" Billy said. He came toward Carrie and enveloped her in a bear hug.

Carrie's body stiffened. *Don't kiss me,* she thought wildly. *Please don't kiss me.*

Billy held her at arms' length and stared into her eyes. "Carrie?" he asked in a low, puzzled voice.

"I just don't want to get your cold," she said quickly.

"I told you, I've already shared my germs with you," he said, and swatted her playfully on the butt. He turned back to the band. "Man, I feet great! I wasn't planning on us doing more than two songs!"

"They sure kept us out there," Pres remarked. "It's nearly ten-thirty."

"Good set, good set," Billy said. "Good job, Sly."

"Thanks," Sly responded, unable to wipe the grin off his face. "I feel . . . I feel terrific!"

Emma and Sam came out of the bathroom, where they had changed out of their stage costumes. Diana was still in there, fixing her makeup.

"We are awesome," Sam sang out, dancing around the tiny dressing room. "They loved us!"

"You got that right," Sly agreed.

"I'm killer thirsty," Sam said. "Who's got a drink?"

Sly offered Sam his can of Coke. Sam took it and was about to raise it to her lips.

"Sam!" Carrie cried out involuntarily.

She can't drink that, Carrie thought. *He has AIDS, and his saliva went in—*

"What?" Sam asked, and then she realized what Carrie meant.

The room got very quiet all of a sudden.

"Oh, nothing," Carrie now said, wildly embarrassed. *I want to die,* she thought. *I want the floor to open up so I can fall through it. . . .*

"Sly, I'm sorry, I—" Carrie began.

Diana had just come out of the bathroom, and witnessed the scene. "Why, Carrie, how politically incorrect of you," she chided, idly running her brush through her hair.

"It's okay, Carrie," Sly said softly, though Carrie knew she saw hurt in his eyes. "No problem. A lot of people react that way."

Carrie managed a sickly smile and then busied herself with her camera case.

Then Billy sneezed. And sneezed again.

"This stupid cold," he remarked. "I can't shake it."

"Singin' all night doesn't help," Pres remarked.

"Singing doesn't give me germs," Billy said crossly, blowing his nose.

"Guys are such babies when they're sick," Diana stated, checking herself in the mirror.

"I'm just not used to it," Billy explained. "I never used to get colds."

Diana turned to him and gave him a sexy look. "Want me to nurse you back to health?"

"No, thanks," Billy replied, packing up his guitar.

"It's just a cold, man," Sly said, with a trace of irony in his voice. "Count your blessings."

Carrie sat down near the dressing table, her camera case in her hands. A horrible, horrible thought hit her. Like some kind of monster, she could feel the tentacles of fear surrounding her throat and tightening.

Dear God. What if it's not just a cold? she thought with rising panic. *That's why I didn't want Billy to kiss me. What if Billy is really sick, too? What if Billy has AIDS?*

SEVEN

Carrie had all her camera equipment spread out on her bed—she was removing her film from the photo shoot she'd done at the Flirts' concert the night before—when Chloe stuck her head into Carrie's bedroom. Chloe had on one of her prettiest nightgowns, and the morning Maine sunlight made her look like a little angel.

Except for the chicken pox and pink lotion blotches on her face, of course, Carrie thought, giving the little girl a loving smile.

"Carrie, I'm bored," Chloe announced.

"Tired of being sick, huh, sweetie?" she commiserated.

"Yup," Chloe replied. "It's boring."

"I bet," Carrie said, returning her attention to her camera.

"There's nothing to do," Chloe complained.

"Why don't you go play Nintendo with Ian?" Carrie asked reasonably.

"He's talking on the phone. Again!" Chloe moped, kicking her big toe against Carrie's door over and over.

Probably with Becky Jacobs, Carrie thought. *No, definitely with Becky Jacobs.*

"He'll be done soon," Carrie assured her, her mind still on her film.

"He always wins," Chloe complained, kicking the door again. "Anyway, it's boring."

She's getting cabin fever, Carrie thought. *She's not used to being cooped up sick. And she's still got a while to go. Poor kid.*

"Hey, I got an idea!" Chloe said with excitement.

"What?" Carrie asked.

"Take my picture! That'd be fun."

"You want me to take your picture even though you're sick?" Carrie asked.

"Yup," Chloe said simply.

"Why?"

"So I can see what I look like with chicken packs when I don't have 'em," Chloe explained, with an exasperated look on her face that said it should be obvious to Carrie if she'd only thought about it for a moment.

"That's a good reason," Carrie agreed. And then, a light bulb went on in her mind.

I need some more pictures for my portfolio for Yale, she thought excitedly. *And they're supposed to be photos that are newsworthy. Why don't I do a photo essay on the chicken pox? All the kids have got it. In fact, I can get Sam . . .*

"Okay, Chloe." Carrie smiled. "You've got yourself a deal."

"You'll do it?" the little girl asked excitedly. "Yeah!"

Carrie smiled, amazed at how little it took to keep Chloe happy.

"You're on," Carrie repeated. "I'll meet you in your room in an hour."

"An hour?" Chloe pouted.

"I need to call my assistant in," Carrie explained solemnly. "Every professional model needs an assistant."

Chloe's eyes got huge. "I'm a professional model?"

"You are," Carrie asserted.

"I'm a model! I'm a model!" Chloe yelled, running back to her room. Carrie could only smile as she turned to her telephone, picked it up, and dialed Sam's number.

"That went relatively well," Carrie said as she led Sam downstairs from Chloe's room.

"I can't believe you talked me into this," Sam groused. "A morning photo session on the chicken pox! Don't tell anyone I know."

"It's better than working," Carrie reminded her.

"Can I help it if the twins are sick?" Sam shot back, following Carrie out the Templetons' front door and into the garage.

"Did you tell them to get ready?" Carrie asked, fiddling in her pocketbook for the keys to the Mercedes. "We're doing them next."

"They insisted on picking their own outfits," Sam explained with a shrug. "I can only imagine what they came up with."

They both got into the car and Carrie pulled it out of the Templetons' long driveway. "Chloe looked so cute dressed up as a clown, didn't she?"

"Darling," Sam agreed. "And Ian as a muscle man—very creative, girlfriend."

"Thanks," Carrie said, pulling the car out onto the street.

Sam opened the car window and let the wind rush through her hair. "So, the twins have probably wrapped themselves in Saran Wrap even as we speak." She reached over and turned on the radio, and Graham's newest single, a poignant ballad called "Time Heals Everything," blared out of the speakers.

"Can you believe you actually work for this guy?" Sam yelled to Carrie over the music.

"Hey, I've seen that rock star in his boxer shorts!" Carrie laughed.

"Wow, you could probably sell an exposé about him to one of those tell-all rags and make a mint," Sam yelled back.

"But I'd never do that," Carrie said, turning onto Beachfront Street.

"Okay, then," Sam said, "just tell me how he looks in his boxer shorts."

Carrie grinned at Sam. "The same way he looks in his bathing suit, which you've seen a zillion times."

Sam shook her head. "Honestly, you do not have a kinky bone in your body."

When they arrived at the Jacobses', the twins were already in the living room waiting for them. Carrie had been prepared for almost anything, but not for the outfits that the twins had chosen for themselves.

"Gee," she managed, her jaw dropping open. "You two look . . . uh . . . original."

The twins were dressed in tiny, matching white bikinis, covered with small pink bubbles, almost as if the bikinis themselves had the chicken pox. On their bodies, they'd dabbed pink calamine lotion on each of their eruptions, and the lotion had dried into more pink bubbles.

And they had beatific smiles on their faces.

"Is this to the max, or what?" Allie asked with excitement.

"They're . . . well," Carrie said, searching for words, "different."

"We thought so," Becky agreed.

"Just out of sick curiosity," Sam said, "how did you do the bubbles on the bikinis?"

"It's junk that comes in a tube thing," Allie said. "We found it in our old toy bin from when we were kids."

"And it still makes bubbles," Sam marveled dryly.

"Pretty cool, huh?" Becky said, posing prettily.

"But, of course," Allie hastened to add, "we won't let you take our picture like this."

"Say what?" Sam asked.

"There's more," Becky intoned mysteriously. "Excuse us." The girls ran into the kitchen.

"You know what this is about?" Carrie asked Sam as she unslung a couple of cameras from her neck.

"Maybe the chicken pox has fried their brains," Sam suggested.

"Okay," Becky said, coming back into the living room. "We're ready. Close your eyes."

"What?" Sam asked.

"Close your eyes," Becky repeated.

Sam and Carrie closed their eyes.

"Okay, now open them."

Carrie opened her eyes. She couldn't help herself: she started to laugh uncontrollably.

Becky and Allie were still wearing their bikinis. But now they had put paper bags over their heads with holes cut out where their eyes were. They looked like fans of a really awful football team who go to games with bags over their heads so that no one watching on television can identify them.

"Okay," Sam called, "very funny. Now, take 'em off!"

"Are you kidding?" Allie screeched, her voice muffled by the paper bag. "You think we're gonna have our pictures taken when we're covered with these zitty things so that people know it's *us*?"

"You guys gotta be on drugs," Becky agreed from inside her bag.

Carrie looked at Sam. "I think there's only one thing we can do," she said calmly.

"What's that?" Sam asked.

Carrie picked up a camera and began shooting.

Carrie closed her eyes and enjoyed the feeling of the late afternoon sun caressing her face. *It feels so good to relax,* Carrie thought. But in the back of her mind was the awful, terrifying worry about Billy. She pushed the thought away and turned over onto her stomach.

"Hey, listen to this," she told Emma and Sam, who were with her on the beach. "Ian tells me he was thinking of changing the name of the band."

"To what?" Emma asked, fiddling with the dial of the portable radio they'd brought out with them.

"He wanted to rename Lord White-head and the Zit People to be Lord Pink-bumps and the Pox People," Carrie said. "Becky talked him out of it."

"Good move," Sam said with a laugh. She grabbed a fabric-covered elastic band and stuck her hair up in a ponytail. "After all, the Zit People is so much more commercial a name."

Carrie laughed. "Tell me about it. Anyway, he's healthy enough now to feel bored just hanging out at home, so he's writing a new song."

"Do I dare ask the name of it?" Sam queried, pulling some sunscreen out of her bag.

"'Chicken Pox Rox,'" Carrie managed to get out before rolling over in a fit of laughter. "I swear to God, that's what he calls it!"

"Done the Zit People way, of course," Emma added.

"Look, enough about the kiddies," Sam said, crossing her legs Indian-fashion. "I have big news."

"You saw aliens from the planet Love-tron," Carrie guessed. "They carried you away in a space ship and made you their love goddess."

"Well, yeah," Sam agreed with a straight face, "but that's not what I was going to tell you. Guess who had a very romantic time at the beach with one very fine bass player last night after our gig."

"Diana?" Carrie queried, an innocent look on her face.

"Not to live to tell about it," Sam replied. "It is me! Little old me! And Pres!"

"That's fabulous!" Emma cried.

"So do you want to hear all about it?" Sam asked. "Okay, you forced it out of me," she added without waiting for an answer. "We talked for a long time about being adopted."

"That makes sense," Carrie said, turning down the radio a bit so she could hear better.

"And then we talked about you," Sam added to Carrie, as if she were saying that she had talked with Pres about the weather forecast.

"Me?" Carrie said, her voice squeaking a little.

"Yes," Sam intoned, "O curvaceous one.

You. And Billy. Pres told me that he thinks Billy is going through a really hard time. Because of Sly, and because of the AIDS test and all."

"So am I," Carrie admitted. That terrible, scary feeling washed over her again. "It's, like, since we took that test, and since Sly said he had AIDS, a lot of my romantic feelings are gone."

"That'll change," Emma told Carrie.

"Maybe," Carrie said. She ran her hand nervously through her hair. "You know, I was really, really thinking about making love with Billy. I mean, I dreamed about it, I fantasized about it, and I love him . . ."

"But?" Emma prompted.

"But," Carrie echoed, "now I feel weird even if he just touches me." She buried her head in her hands. "God, that is so awful! How could I?"

"Well, according to Pres, Billy is just as freaked as you are," Sam related. "Only he's a guy, so he wants to hide it more."

"I sometimes wish we never even went for the AIDS tests!" Carrie cried bitterly.

"Carrie, whether you went for the tests or not, Sly would have come back," Emma reminded her friend. "And you would have been upset just the same."

"Pres said that the test doesn't matter, really," Sam said.

"Unless it's positive," Carrie reminded them in an unhappy voice.

"Unless it's positive," Emma echoed.

"For either of you," Sam said.

"Don't you think it's best to just not know?" Carrie asked, feeling that same panic she'd felt the night before. "There's nothing doctors can do, anyway."

"That's not true," Emma said, picking up a copy of *Time* magazine she had in her beachbag. "An article in here says there are some new early therapies—"

"They don't cure you," Carrie replied heatedly. "Otherwise, Sly would be healthy, right?"

The girls were silent for a moment. Carrie was partly right.

Emma finally spoke in measured tones. "Look Carrie," she said, "you're getting all worked up over nothing. You're both going to be negative. I just know it!"

"Look at all the rock stars who've had

sex with anything that walked!" Sam spoke up. "They're negative."

Carrie sighed. *They're right, I know they're right. But I keep thinking about Billy and that other girl, and the condom breaking, and . . . everything!*

"You guys are lucky," Carrie said finally.

"Why's that?" Emma asked.

"You don't have boyfriends," Carrie answered, feeling uncharacteristically sorry for herself. She sat up. "I mean, this really, really sucks. I love Billy! But even if the tests are negative, I don't know if I'm going to sleep with him."

Emma smiled. "Your parents would approve, anyway."

"Not necessarily," Carrie replied. "My parents always taught me that sex was something very special that belonged in the context of a loving, committed relationship. They never said I should or shouldn't wait until I got married."

"Well, my parents never discussed it with me at all," Emma said bitterly. "Can you imagine Kat telling me not to have sex? But I always knew I never wanted to be like her—maybe that's one of the reasons I'm still a virgin."

"Now, my parental units gave me the old-fashioned you-get-married-in-white-for-a-reason lecture," Sam said. "But, hey, they're from Kansas."

"I hate to break it to you, Sam," Carrie said, "but that attitude isn't limited to Kansas."

"I know," Sam agreed. "Scary, isn't it?"

"Ha," Emma said. "You talk so tough, but I notice you haven't taken the big plunge."

Sam lay down on her back and put her hands under her head. She stared up at the sky. "Sometimes I think it sounds so romantic, you know? Being a virgin on your wedding night." She looked over at her friends. "And then other times I think, 'What are you, Sam, nuts?' Especially since I don't even think I ever want to get married. Which means I would die the oldest known virgin! They'd put me in the *Guinness Book of World Records!*"

"We already know you're nuts," Carrie said. "As for the other part—well, I guess that's something we each have to decide for ourselves, huh?"

"As opposed to the parental units," Sam translated.

"Right," Carrie agreed with a sigh. "Sometimes being a grown-up just sucks the big one."

"Well, let me say this," Sam stated with importance. "Pres and I got a lot closer last night."

Carrie raised her eyebrows. "Just how close?"

"You sound like me," Sam told her. "What I mean is, we talked. Really talked. For a long time." She looked at Carrie. "Which is what I think you need to do with Billy." Sam reached for her sunglasses and resettled them on her head.

"That's a very mature attitude," Carrie told Sam.

"Yep, that's me—very, very mature!" Sam agreed. She grinned at her friends. "I might add that Pres kissed me goodnight. And I mean he *kissed* me—yowza!"

Emma reached out and touched Carrie's hand. "Sam's right, you know. You're really upset—we can see that. You should talk it over more with Billy, don't you think?"

Carrie lay down and stared at the wooly clouds crossing the sky. A bird swooped up and made a lazy arc against the sun. "Yeah," she finally said. "I do."

EIGHT

"Billy?" Carrie spoke quietly into the phone.

"Yeah?"

"It's Carrie."

"Hi, babe."

Carrie leaned back on her bed and propped the phone up against her ear. She glanced at her bedside clock, which read 12:05 A.M. She'd spent the entire evening with Emma and Sam—after the afternoon at the beach, they'd ended up going to Portland to see a movie and walking around Front Street, window-shopping. She and her friends had been so distracted, they were lucky to catch the last ferry back to the island.

When Carrie got back to the Templetons' house, all the lights were out. Even Claudia, who sometimes suffered from insomnia, was asleep.

I'm tired, too, Carrie thought. *But I want so much to talk to Billy, even if I'm not sure what I want to say to him! I know I should wait until morning, but I don't want to wait!*

Finally, she took a quick shower and put on the old Yale T-shirt she usually slept in. Her mind was still not made up. Then she got in bed, stared at the phone, and finally dialed Billy's number.

"I was hoping you'd answer," Carrie said. "I know it's late. I'm sorry."

"Look, you know you can call me anytime," Billy said to her warmly. "Actually, I was lying here in my lonely bed thinking about you, anyway."

"That's nice," Carrie replied, noticing a crescent moon through her window. "I hope you're not mad at me or anything."

"Why would I be mad at you?" Billy asked.

"I can think of a few reasons," Carrie said quietly. "Like when I didn't want

116

you to kiss me backstage. Like what happened with Sly. I was such an idiot!"

"I haven't thought about it since," Billy replied, and Carrie could tell from the sound of his voice that he was telling the truth.

Carrie nervously wrapped and then unwrapped the phone cord around her left forefinger. "I . . . I still feel bad, though—"

"Forget it," Billy said. "It didn't mean anything. You didn't mean anything by it."

Do I dare tell him the truth? Carrie asked herself. *What will happen if I tell him the total truth?*

"I want to talk to you about something," she began slowly, "but . . . I'm sort of afraid to."

"Why?"

"Because it might make you mad."

"Carrie—" Billy's voice was comforting and soothing "—the drummer in my band—my good friend—has full-blown AIDS. He's twenty years old and he's going to die in the next few years. Now, *that* makes me mad. But nothing you're going to say to me is going to make me mad unless you say you don't love me anymore."

"I do love you," Carrie said fervently, and she knew it was true as she said it.

"Then, what?" Billy asked.

"Okay," Carrie replied, turning off the light in her room and lying back on the bed in the dark, still holding the telephone. When she talked, it was as if Billy was lying next to her.

"Okay, what?" Billy prompted.

"When you touched me, when you went to kiss me . . ." Carrie took a deep breath. "I didn't want you to. And it wasn't because you have a cold. Something scared me."

There, I've said it, Carrie thought. *Now, I hope he's as good as his word.*

"What part scared you?"

"That you might have AIDS," Carrie answered, her voice barely a whisper.

"Carrie," Billy answered, "we are going to find out the day after tomorrow that I don't have AIDS, and that you don't have AIDS. And then all of this will be behind us."

118

"But you were so worried about taking the test," Carrie cried. "And then you told me about your old girlfriend and what happened with her, and now Sly has it. Did Sly sleep with that girl, too?"

"Of course not!" Billy exploded.

Carrie kicked at her coverlet with agitation. "I just . . . I feel so nervous! So awful!"

"Carrie—"

"I know I'm being irrational, and I know it isn't like me—you don't have to tell me," Carrie said.

"So I won't," Billy said. He sighed. "Look, Car, I can't tell you I haven't been thinking about it too, because I have. But we're probably both worried about nothing—"

"You've had so many colds lately," Carrie interrupted. "That's a sign your immune system isn't good."

"Carrie," Billy reasoned, his voice still calm, "haven't you ever had two colds in a row? Or even three?"

"Yes, but—"

"But nothing," Billy said firmly. "I'm taking vitamin C and I'll be fine."

"Billy?" Carrie asked in a quiet voice.

"Yes?"

"If . . ." Carrie began, then stopped. "Wow, this is really hard to say." She took a deep breath. "If I don't want us to make love even if our tests are both negative, what will you think?"

"What will I think?" Billy repeated.

"Uh-huh."

"Why?" Billy asked. "Is that what you've decided?"

"I don't know," Carrie replied. "I'm all confused! I don't know what I've decided!"

"Well, I think . . . I think that I'd respect what you want to do," Billy replied.

"Would you still want to make love with me?" Carrie asked him in a low voice.

"Of course," he told her. "Car, I love you. We've been together a long time now. We're committed to each other. As far as I'm concerned, two adults in love—in a long-term, committed relationship—make love. It's natural. It's healthy."

"You make it sound so simple," Carrie said. "But it doesn't feel simple at all."

"Look, you know I won't pressure you," Billy said. "But I believe what I believe. I'm not gonna change that to suit anyone else's sense of morality. I mean, this is something we decide together."

"So . . . you wouldn't be angry with me?"

"Carrie," Billy said softly, "this is the age of AIDS. I already told you what makes me angry. And it's not Carrie Alden."

"Chloe, cut it out!" Ian yelled, his voice carrying all the way downstairs.

"No!" Chloe yelled back. "I'm not doing anything!"

"*Ma!*" Ian cried. "She's looking at me—tell her to stop looking at me. I'm trying to work in here!"

Claudia took a sip of coffee and shook her head wearily. Carrie sipped hers, too, and gave her employer an understanding shrug. The two of them were having a late breakfast. It was the morning after

Carrie's phone call with Billy, and she'd slept later than usual.

"Apparently," Claudia said, a bemused look on her face, "the natives are getting restless."

"Apparently." Carrie smiled back.

"Doctor Mullins says at least six more days, maybe seven." Claudia sighed. "I can't wait. I'm only hoping one won't kill the other before then."

"*Maaa!*" Ian yelled again at the top of his lungs.

"On second thought," Claudia said, "maybe they could both kill each other and we'd have some peace."

"Chloe's bugging me," Ian yelled. "I'm trying to make art here. Tell her to quit looking at me!"

"Quit looking!" Claudia yelled, not even bothering to look up. "Chloe, leave your brother alone."

Miraculously, there was silence from the top of the stairs.

"Six days," Claudia repeated.

"I'll be around," Carrie promised, "between now and then." She reached over, took a fresh peach from the fruit bowl on the table, and bit into it.

"Good," Claudia replied, reaching for some grapes. "Maybe you could read Chloe a story or something."

"Sure," Carrie agreed. "I can handle that."

Ian came bounding down the stairs. "Check out my song, Mom," he said, a beaming grin on his face. He was wearing a pair of black jeans and a white sweatshirt with his father's name and band logo embroidered on it, and he looked extremely cute, even with the chicken pox marks on his face.

"Can I hear it, too?" Carrie asked, trying to be helpful to Claudia.

"Sure, Carrie," Ian said. "Remember, though, it's still a work-in-progress."

He just won't quit, Carrie marveled. *The kid's got his heart set on being a musician and songwriter like his father. It's just too bad he doesn't have Graham's talent. Well, maybe he'll be a late bloomer.*

Claudia smiled her most encouraging smile at her son. Carrie knew that Claudia had a similar opinion of Ian's level of talent, but that she would do whatever she could to keep the boy's self-esteem up.

It's tough being the child of a rock star, Carrie mused. *Everyone thinks you must have the greatest life, but they forget that you never asked for your father to be famous.*

"I'll recite it," Ian said.

"I thought was a song," Claudia reminded him.

"It's a talking blues, kind of like classic Bob Dylan, but meant to be done the Zit People way, of course," Ian explained seriously.

I think that's the first time Bob Dylan and the Zit People have ever been mentioned in the same sentence, Carrie thought, grinning to herself. *I hope I can keep a straight face.*

"What's the title?" Carrie asked.

"'Chicken Pox Rox,'" Ian replied. "It goes something like this." Here, Ian picked up a spatula that was leaning in the sink, grabbed the handle part of it so that the flat plastic part was up by his mouth, and started bopping around the room as he recited:

It's an odd kind of plague
that strikes when you're a kid—
and it gives itchy scratchies
you wish you were a squid!
So you could take your tentacles
and wind them around
each one of those eruptions
that are getting you down!
Chicken Pox Rox, Chicken Pox Rox,
Lord Whitehead and the Zits
got the Chicken Pox Rox.

Ian stopped reciting. "That's the first verse and chorus, of course," he said.

"Of course," Carrie replied.

"It's original," Claudia said encouragingly.

"The performance concept is that at the chorus," Ian explained, his eyes shining, "we'd all run to the front of the stage and scratch ourselves uncontrollably. I think it makes a statement."

"Uh-huh," Carrie agreed carefully.

"It'd be great for, like, a little kid's

birthday party kind of a gig," he continued. "There's a lot of business in doing birthday parties."

"Uh-huh," Carrie said again.

"I think you're humoring me," Ian said, looking Carrie straight in the eye.

What? Carrie thought. *Well, I'm busted.* "Sorry, Ian, I—"

"That's okay," Ian interrupted, with no malice in his voice. "It's a kid thing. You wouldn't understand."

NINE

"So," Emma began, as she and Carrie drove together toward the Flirts' house, "you get your AIDS test results tomorrow, right?"

"Five o'clock," Carrie replied nervously, turning the corner. "I can't tell you how much I'm looking forward to it."

"I know," Emma said, touching her friend on the shoulder. "This hasn't been easy for you."

"It's been hell, actually," Carrie replied, pulling the car into the driveway. "But at least it'll finally be over. And everything can go back to normal." She thought about Sly. "Well, as normal as it can be, anyway," she added.

"So you have any idea what this band meeting is about?" Emma asked Carrie.

"Not a clue," Carrie replied. "But Billy asked me to come."

"If he wants you there," Emma thought aloud, "I bet it's something to do with Sly."

"Probably," Carrie agreed with a sigh. She looked over at her friend. "Don't you wish things could just go back to how they used to be?"

Emma nodded. "I hope everything's okay."

"Me, too."

Carrie turned off the car and the two of them sat there for a moment. *I hope it isn't terrible news,* Carrie thought to herself. *I can't take any more terrible news.*

"So what happens with your AIDS test?" Emma asked, turning to Carrie. "Do you just call the doctor and he tells you?"

"*She* tells us, in this case," Carrie replied. "And no, we can't do it by phone. Doctor Mullins wants us to come in and see her again."

"I wonder why," Emma mused. "There isn't anything wrong, is there?"

"I wondered the same thing," Carrie

replied nervously, taking the keys out of the ignition.

"Maybe that's how they always do it?" Emma ventured.

Carrie nodded. "She said she only gives AIDS test results in person."

"That's probably a good idea," Emma said. "I mean, what if you've actually got it? Do you really want to find out by phone?"

"I don't really want to find out at all," Carrie said, opening her car door. They walked toward the house.

"You know," Carrie continued, "I told Billy I wasn't sure about us making love even if the tests are negative."

"What did he say to that?" Emma asked, her voice a little surprised. "But it's good you told him," she added quickly.

"He said he'd respect my decision," Carrie reported.

"Did he say anything about what he wanted?" Emma asked.

"Yes," Carrie answered. "You know what he wanted."

"I hope that doesn't get to be a problem," Emma said.

"Me, neither," Carrie mused. "Me, neither."

Actually, Carrie thought, *the more I think about it, the more that part of my conversation with Billy really scares me. Why wouldn't he want another girlfriend, one who would have sex with him? But no, Billy isn't like that. He isn't!*

"It looks like Sam's here already," Emma commented, spotting Sam's bicycle, which she had borrowed from the Jacobs family, parked on the front porch. Recently, Sam had been using the bike to get around a lot, instead of driving. She said it was good for her legs, and also that she liked the male attention from passersbys while she rode around.

"She's starting to hang out more with Pres again," Carrie noted.

"Yes," Emma said neutrally, measuring her words. "I'm happy for her."

If she's happy for Sam, Carrie thought, studying Emma's profile, *that's the most unenthusiastic expression of happiness I've ever heard. I remember that for a while during the Flirts' tour, Emma and Pres were hanging out a lot, when Sam was doing all that flirting with Johnny Angel. Is it possible that Emma's actually jealous? Perfect Emma?*

Carrie let the thought drop as she rang the doorbell. Billy answered it, and the two of them embraced for a quick moment.

"You feel good," Carrie told him in a low voice.

"You, too, babe," Billy whispered into her ear.

Then he ushered the two of them into the living room, where the band had met so often before to go over business.

"Everyone's already here," Billy noted.

"You're sure you guys all want me here?" Carrie asked. She couldn't quite meet Sly's gaze.

"We want you," Sly said, a warm smile on his face.

"Wouldn't have it any other way," Billy insisted. "You're our secret weapon." He leaned close to Carrie. "Hey, can I talk to you out in the hall for a minute?"

"Sure," she said, a feeling of trepidation coming over her.

"We'll be right back," he called in to the

band, and then he walked back into the hall with Carrie.

Is everything okay? Carrie thought. *What does he need to talk to me alone for? It's about the AIDS test—I know it is. Dr. Mullins called him!*

"Car—" Billy began.

"It's about the AIDS test," Carrie said quietly. "I know."

"Did Dr. Mullins call you, too?" Billy asked her.

"No," Carrie answered, her heart pounding in her chest. "She called you?"

"Yes," Billy replied.

Oh, God, here comes the worst thing in the world, Carrie thought to herself. *How will I ever be able to handle this? World, get ready to watch Carrie Alden fall apart before your very eyes.*

"You've got it," Carrie mumbled.

"What?" Billy asked.

"AIDS," Carrie said, barely breathing. "The tests came back and you've got it. But why did she call you? She said she didn't give results over the phone and—"

Billy started to laugh. And then he started to laugh harder and harder and harder. He could barely compose himself to speak. "No," he sputtered, "the office didn't call me to tell me I had it. They called to say that our test results won't be in until tomorrow!"

Billy and Carrie looked at each other. Then they cracked up together and fell into each other's arms for a long, warm hug.

"This is taking all the fun out of romance, you know," Carrie commented.

"I know," Billy answered. "I know it. Come on, we'd better get inside. They're about to send out a search party."

Hand in hand, Billy and Carrie made their way into the Flirts' living room.

Sam, Pres, Jay, Diana, and Sly were all sprawled out around the living room, talking quietly. Carrie quickly saw that Sam and Pres were sitting together on the brown loveseat. She saw that Emma noticed, too, but if it upset her, Carrie couldn't tell. Jay was telling a story about some fiddle player he'd met who picked up girls by saying he could teach them to play the violin in an hour. Alone. In his hotel room.

Billy crossed the room and sat in his usual place on the couch. "Let's get started, gang." Everyone quieted down. Billy turned to Sly.

"It's your ballgame, big guy," Billy told him. "Do what you gotta do."

Sly stood up. He looked thin in his plain white T-shirt and old blue jeans, but when he spoke his voice was clear and full of purpose.

"I'll skip the prelims," Sly said, a thin grin on his face. "I asked Billy to call this meeting because I wanted you guys to be the first to know that I've decided to come out."

"Come out?" Diana yelped, unable to stop herself from choking as she spoke. "You mean you really *are* gay?"

Sly laughed. "That's not what I'm talking about, Diana," he said. "What I mean is that I'm going to be up-front about having AIDS."

"Most of the kids on the island already know," Diana said, "or they wouldn't have donated all that money to Maine CARES at our gig." She caught Sly's look. "Oh, you mean, like, to the whole world? Publicly?"

"Is there any other way?" Sly replied. "Or should I just be up-front here on this little, insignificant island?"

"No need to get testy," Diana replied. "It's just that—"

"Look," Sly said, "it's bad enough I have this stupid disease. I'm not going to hide it from the world. What good would that do?"

Oh boy, Carrie thought. *This is going to get interesting in a hurry. Does Sly know what he's getting himself into? Everyone is going to assume he's gay. Not that what they assume matters, of course.*

"You gonna tell people how you got it?" Diana queried.

"That's not the issue," Sly replied. "The issue is that I got it. I'm not even sure how I got it."

"People are gonna want to know," Diana pointed out.

"Too bad," Sly said.

"Well, I hope you know everyone is going to think you're gay now," Diana continued.

"Well, that's just too damn bad, too," Sly said, folding his arms.

"And they're gonna ask you," Diana pressed on. "And what are you going to say?"

"Exactly what I'm saying to you," Sly said in an even voice. "That it's irrelevant."

"Sly isn't gay," Jay put in. "I've known the guy, like, forever!"

"No, I'm not," Sly said quietly. "And that's the very last time we're gonna deal with that issue."

"Cool," Pres agreed. "Folks are jus' gonna have to deal. It's up to you, man."

Billy jumped in. "Sly talked with me about this before the meeting," he said. "We've prepared a press release for the local papers."

"Not really a release," Sly clarified. "A statement. The party line, so to speak. In case anyone asks. Which they most certainly will." He reached down and picked up several sheets of paper, which he passed around the room. Carrie held onto one, looked down, and read it. It was a mere three paragraphs long, but it spoke volumes.

FLIRTING WITH DANGER
—BAND STATEMENT—

Flirting With Danger drummer Sly Smith, age 20, was recently diagnosed with Acquired Immunodeficiency Syndrome (AIDS).

Smith, one of the original members of the band, continues to drum with them and will be the band's drummer in the foreseeable future. A substitute temporarily took his place during a recent AIDS-related hospitalization, but Smith returned to Sunset Island and the band several days ago.

AIDS continues to be a deadly disease, affecting young and old, men and women alike. It is the hope of the band that medical science will soon find a cure. It is the hope of Smith that, by continuing as the band's drummer, he can prove people with AIDS are not outcasts and can lead full, productive lives as long as their health permits.

Carrie couldn't help it: tears rolled down her face as she read the release.

Oh, great, she thought. *What's everyone going to think of me now?*

Then she heard snuffling from around the room. She looked from face to face. Not only were Emma and Sam crying, but so were the guys. Even Diana had tears in her eyes.

The only person not crying was Sly.

"Hey!" he yelled, smacking his hands together. "Ready for 'Love Junkie'?" He pulled a couple of drumsticks out of his back pocket and strode over to the coffee table, where he began to beat the opening riff on the wooden tabletop.

Pres immediately saw what he was doing, bounded across the room, pulled on his guitar, and started ramming out the rhythm cords.

And then the band sang "Love Junkie" like never before—no mikes, no costumes, no instruments other than Pres on the bass guitar.

And all of them agreed afterward that they had never sounded better.

"You know," Carrie said to Billy as they drove together to Dr. Mullins's office the next day, "I don't feel nearly so weird as I did a few days ago."

"Yeah?" Billy asked. "Well, give the credit to Sly, I'd say."

"That was amazing yesterday afternoon," Carrie agreed as Billy headed the car down Main Street toward the small professional center where Dr. Mullins had her office.

"I know," Billy commented. "He's got a lot of courage."

"He's changed," Carrie said. "He's, well . . . nicer."

"I know," Billy replied.

"Do you think he had to get AIDS to get nice?" Carrie queried.

"God, I hope not," Billy answered philosophically, "but don't forget, Sly has known about it for a while. I'm sure keeping that a secret wasn't helping his disposition."

"I guess not," Carrie agreed. She stared out the window at the passing scenery. "I guess he had a choice. He could rise to this test, or not."

"Yeah," Billy agreed. "I'm proud of him." He looked over at Carrie. "I only hope I'd handle it as well."

The traffic was fairly heavy with cars coming back from the main beach, and Billy and Carrie inched along slowly.

"You know," Carrie said, "I'm not dead set against us sleeping together if the tests come back negative."

"That's good"—Billy grinned—"because I'm not, either." The two of them laughed.

"We'll just have to see," Carrie continued.

I'm so glad we're finally getting this over with, Carrie thought. *I'm going to be so glad to find out that Billy's fine, and that I'm fine, too.*

"Aw, c'mon," Billy joked. "There's no way you're going to be able to resist my incredible, perfect physique."

Carrie pretended to gag herself, and they both laughed.

Billy finally pulled his van into the driveway of the professional center, and hand in hand they made their way into Dr.

Mullins's office. They signed the check-in sheet and sat down. The office was not quite as crowded as the time before, and it seemed like there were fewer kids there with the chicken pox.

Finally, the doctor's administrative assistant called their names.

"Carrie Alden? Billy Sampson?"

Carrie and Billy approached the glass window behind which she was seated.

"We're Sampson and Alden," Billy said in a firm voice.

"Oh, you'll have to wait a while longer. The lab hasn't delivered your test results," said the assistant, a middle-aged woman with brown hair done up in a neat bun. "Just have a seat."

"Hurry up and wait, huh?" Billy muttered to Carrie as they sat back down. For lack of anything better to do, they started playing a game of checkers that had been left out for waiting kids. After about twenty minutes, a man in a delivery-truck uniform came in, went to the assistant's window, and handed her an official-looking envelope. By this time, they were the only two people left in the waiting room.

"That's us," Billy said.

Carrie nodded. Her stomach felt as if she were dropping off the top of a roller coaster.

And I was feeling so calm there for a while, she realized. *Well, this is finally it. . . .*

A few minutes later, the assistant came out to usher both of them into Dr. Mullins's office. Carrie followed Billy in.

Oh, my God, Carrie thought. *She's really pale. What's wrong?*

"Sit down, please," Dr. Mullins said, her voice almost too controlled.

"There's something wrong. I know there's something wrong," Carrie blurted out, unable to contain herself. "Oh, my God, one of us has AIDS!"

Dr. Mullins slowly shook her head. "It's not the AIDS test. You're both negative."

A huge grin spread across Billy's face. "See? I told you there was nothing—"

"Billy," Dr. Mullins said slowly, "there is a problem with one of your other tests."

"Mine?" Billy asked, looking confused.

"Yes," Dr. Mullins said. "You know we did a complete blood workup on you, since you said you haven't been feeling well and you've been having so many colds. . . ."

"Yeah," Billy said in a barely audible voice. Carrie grabbed his hand and squeezed it hard. Both of them were shaking violently.

"We're going to need to get you admitted to Maine Medical Center. Right away," Dr. Mullins insisted. "I believe you may have leukemia."

TEN

"It's okay, Billy," Carrie said in as soothing voice as she could muster. "It's going to be okay."

Billy turned to her, a look of pure terror on his face. He opened his mouth to speak, but no words came out.

I can't believe this is happening, Carrie thought to herself. *Please, God, let me wake up from this terrible nightmare.*

But Carrie didn't wake up. And everything was all too real. She walked across the room at the Maine Medical Center and stared out the window at the park across the street. *How can everything out there look the same, when my life and Billy's life are being torn apart?* Carrie thought about the most recent time she'd been in the hospital: when Emma's father had had a heart attack.

And I remember then that I vowed to stay out of hospitals, I hate them so much. Now here I am, my boyfriend's got tubes in him, and we're just waiting for some tests to be repeated before he has to get a bone marrow biopsy and then start chemotherapy.

Carrie used all her willpower to keep herself from crying. She knew Billy needed her to be strong. So she took a deep breath and turned back to her boyfriend.

"Are Emma and Sam here?" Billy asked, his voice slightly dreamy.

Good, Carrie thought gratefully. *He sounds more relaxed. That means that the tranquilizer Dr. Mullins prescribed for him is starting to work.*

"They're in the waiting room downstairs," Carrie answered, sitting in the chair next to Billy's bed. "They thought we might want to be alone."

"To do what?" Billy answered, a trace of medication-tempered bitterness in his voice. "Don't answer that—I didn't mean it."

Carrie just squeezed his hand. She thought back over the awful hours since they'd sat together in Dr. Mullins' office. The doctor had wanted him admitted to the hospital right away, so that the lab could run some confirming tests and so they could they could do a bone marrow biopsy if the tests confirmed the diagnosis. Then, they'd begin chemotherapy immediately, if necessary. The doctor had talked to Billy all about leukemia—a cancer of the blood—and told him that the prognosis would very much depend on how far along his disease was.

"Some people with leukemia," she'd said, "actually make a complete recovery."

"Others die," Billy had said glumly. The doctor did not disagree.

Dr. Mullins had called the Maine Medical Center, where she spoke to a variety of people over the course of about twenty minutes, including the chief resident of the oncology—cancer—department. Then, Dr. Mullins asked whether

Billy had anyone he wanted to contact before he got his things together to go into the hospital.

Billy had looked at Carrie, and Carrie had seen pure fright in his eyes. "My parents," he'd said with the expression of a zombie.

Dr. Mullins had kindly pushed the telephone over to him.

"I'll stay here," she'd said. "They may want to speak to me."

Billy had nodded. That was when Carrie lost it. Tears began streaming down her cheeks. Neither Dr. Mullins nor Billy had made any effort to stop her, other than for the doctor to offer her a box of tissues that occupied a convenient corner of her desk.

Finding Billy's parents was an ordeal. First Billy had called their home in Seattle, but the message on the answering machine told him to call a travel agency to get their itinerary—they were on vacation in Canada. Finally, after numerous phone calls, Billy tracked his folks down at a fishing camp in northern Ontario. And then he called them to utter the most horrible set of words that Carrie had ever heard.

"Mom?" Billy had said. "I'm calling you from a doctor's office on Sunset Island. They think I may have leukemia."

The conversation, Carrie remembered, had been awful. Billy's parents were going to cut short their vacation immediately, of course, but they were so far back in the woods that a float plane would have to be called in for fast transportation, they'd have to fly to Toronto, and then to Boston, and then to Portland. There was no way they'd be there for twelve hours at least, and possibly not for a whole day.

The rest of the evening had passed in a total blur: going home to the Flirts' house to get Billy's belongings, leaving a note for the rest of the guys, who were out in Portland seeing a movie—at a theater two blocks from the hospital, Carrie recalled bitterly—calling Claudia, and then calling Emma and Sam, who said they'd meet Carrie at the hospital. Then, the ferry ride and terrible drive to the Maine Medical Center in Portland. She looked around the semi-private room on the second floor of the hospital. It looked like any other antiseptic hospital room she'd ever been in, with the same institutionally painted walls, the same remote-control television sticking out from the wall, the same metal-framed hospital bed with white sheets, the same nurse call-button over the bed.

But this time her boyfriend was the one in the bed, with a clear intravenous drip going into his arm. And Carrie was more frightened than she'd ever been in her life. But she couldn't let Billy see that fear.

At least there's no one sharing the room with him, Carrie thought. *Yet. I think that would depress him even more. And me. I wish that nurse who was here before had offered me one of those Valiums. I probably would have taken it if she did.*

"What about Pres? And Jay? And Sly?" Billy asked.

"We left a note for them at the house, remember?"

"Oh, yeah," Billy said, leaning back

into his pillow. "Sorry." He rubbed his eyes. "I must be losing it."

"It's probably just the Valium," Carrie assured him. "How do you feel?"

"Like this is a nightmare, but I can't wake myself up," Billy replied.

Carrie nodded in agreement.

"How can this be possible?" Billy asked her, his eyes searching her face for answers. "I mean, nothing hurts. I have a cold, that's all. Isn't something that's going to kill you supposed to hurt?"

Carrie felt like someone was stabbing her in her heart. "Billy, leukemia isn't a death sentence," she said firmly. "It's not like it used to be."

"Since when do you know so much about it?" he asked her bitterly.

"Well, I don't," Carrie admitted. "But I listened to what Doctor Mullins said. And I've read enough to know that lots of people live through leukemia. They go into remission. They get well!"

"And lots don't," Billy added in a low voice. His eyes searched her face again. "Do you think Doctor Mullins could be wrong?"

"Well, she didn't say for sure. . . ." Carrie hedged.

Their eyes met. The odds that it was all a big error seemed remote at best.

Billy leaned over and gently brushed some hair off of Carrie's face. "How's my girl doing?" he asked softly.

The fact that Billy was able to think about her feelings at that moment filled her heart with love, and she managed a small smile. "Okay," she fibbed. "As well as you'd expect."

A very pretty white-clad young nurse with a long red braid down her back stuck her head in the door.

"You doing okay?" she asked Billy in a chirpy voice.

He nodded tersely.

"Just call if you need anything," the nurse said warmly.

"I need a new life," Billy responded.

"I'm sure that's how you feel," the nurse said. "I can call the hospital counselor if you want to talk to someone."

"Right now," Billy said, "the only person I want to talk to is in the room with me." He squeezed Carrie's hand.

"I understand," the nurse replied. "Well, call me if you need anything else. My name is Gina, by the way." She glanced around the room, walked over and gave a quick inspection to Billy's IV tubes, and then left.

"She's really pretty, huh?" Carrie commented, trying to make conversation.

Billy attempted a smile. "If I was healthy, you would never be pointing out how pretty another girl is."

Carrie couldn't respond to that, because he was right.

"I hope they're done taking blood," Billy said. "That was torture."

Right after Billy had gotten into his room, the chief resident, a black doctor in his mid-30s named Dr. Lowe, had come in and drawn the blood that would be used to repeat Billy's blood tests. He told Billy in a matter-of-fact voice that they'd be looking at Billy's blood count, to see the number of white blood cells in it. In the test that Dr. Mullins had done, Dr. Lowe explained, there were lots of immature forms of white blood cells—a big warning sign of leukemia.

"What we need to do now is repeat the tests, and some others, and see what we see."

"How soon until I get the results?" Billy had asked him.

"Tomorrow," the doctor had said. "If the results look bad, we'll have to do a bone marrow biopsy." Dr. Lowe went on to explain that this was a procedure where the doctors punched an instrument into the hipbone and cored out a piece of bone marrow to study.

"Does it hurt?" Billy asked.

"It doesn't tickle," the doctor had said honestly.

"Great," Billy had responded. "Let the fun begin."

Dr. Lowe had patted Billy's arm. "Did Doctor Mullins tell you about chemotherapy?"

"Yup," Billy answered. "Sounds like more fun and games. Lots of throwing up and then my hair falls out. I've got a lot to look forward to."

"Attitude is everything," Dr. Lowe had cautioned.

"Right now," Billy had muttered, "mine sucks."

"I hope it improves," Dr. Lowe said, the gravity of his words etched across his face. "I know all of this is sudden, and I can imagine how difficult it is. But time and again I have seen people with a positive attitude rally, while people with a defeatist attitude got sicker. The mind and the body are very closely connected— probably in more ways than we can begin to understand."

"Next you'll be telling me I gave myself leukemia because I'm not a positive-thinking person," Billy said sardonically.

"Not at all," Dr. Lowe said. "I'm talking about how you deal with whatever it is we discover. Just keep that in mind." Then he'd patted Billy's arm again and excused himself to continue his evening rounds.

Carrie pulled herself out of her recollection and forced herself to focus back on Billy and the conversation at hand.

"Maybe the test results are wrong," Carrie tried feebly.

"Maybe the world is really flat," Billy

replied. "You know what the crazy part is?" he asked, his voice getting a little more dreamy from the Valium.

"What?" Carrie asked.

"That we were all worried," Billy answered, his voice faraway. "We were worried sick. And it turned out that we were worried about the wrong thing."

"Yeah," Carrie answered.

"That's weird," Billy murmured, "really weird."

"Yeah," Carrie said again.

This time, Billy didn't answer. The Valium had finally done its job. Billy had fallen asleep. Carrie got up, kissed him lightly on the forehead, turned out the lights in the room, and padded out as quietly as she could.

I hope Emma and Sam are waiting for me in the cafeteria, Carrie thought. *Because I need someone to help me fall apart, and I can't think of two better shoulders to cry on.*

"Hi," Sam said in a subdued voice, as Carrie made her way into the nearly deserted cafeteria. "Pull up a chair."

"How is he?" Emma asked.

"Sleeping," Carrie replied, slipping into the chair that Sam had pulled out for her. She put her head down on the table wearily.

Emma stroked Carrie's hair. "God, this is so . . ." She searched for the right words. "It's too horrible to even call 'horrible,' isn't it?"

Carrie nodded from underneath her hair.

"Even I won't joke about it," Sam promised.

Carrie lifted her head. "Thanks," she said wearily. "I'm not up for humor yet."

"You know," Emma said, "I could go call my mother. She's knows all kinds of specialists in Boston—"

Carrie cut her off with a wave of her hand. "Let's wait until tomorrow," she said. "Billy's blood tests will be back and . . . well, I guess we'll deal with it then."

"Do the doctors really think he has leukemia?" Sam asked.

Carrie nodded.

"God." Sam drew in her breath quickly.

"And I thought the chicken pox was bad."
She clapped her hand quickly over her
mouth.

Carrie managed a quick grin. "It's okay,"
she assured her friend. "I thought the
chicken pox was bad, too."

"Can we get you anything?" Emma
asked. "Have you eaten?"

"The last thing I'm thinking about is
food," Carrie said with exhaustion. "Actually, how about a cup of coffee?"

Emma nodded, got up, and went to the
cafeteria line. Sam and Carrie sat together silently. When Emma came back
with Carrie's coffee, Carrie started to fill
them in on the story of the visit to Dr.
Mullins's office, leading right up to
Billy's admittance to the hospital. As she
talked, her voice got more and more glum.

"So that's the story," she concluded.
"And it really, really sucks."

"I feel terrible for you," Emma said.

"I feel terrible for myself," Carrie
agreed. "And I really feel terrible for
Billy. He's so scared. I've never seen him
like this."

"Well, he's never had to face anything like this before," Emma pointed out.

"Neither have I," Carrie admitted. She gave a small, bitter smile. "I remember how scared I was when I thought I was going to have to marry my friend Raymond Saliverez. And remember that hurricane on the island? I was petrified then. Or the time we got lost at sea in that little dinghy. . . ." Carrie had a faraway look in her eyes, then she focused back on her friends. "But now I wonder, what was I so afraid of? Because it couldn't hold a candle to how I feel right now."

"I remember how scared I was when my father had his heart attack," Emma recalled in a soft voice.

"It's kind of the same thing," Carrie observed. "This must be close to what you were going through."

"I'm sick of people getting sick!" Sam exclaimed passionately. "Emma's dad, Sly, Billy—"

"We don't know if Billy is sick yet," Emma said firmly. "He just had some bad test results."

"Emma, the tests don't lie," Sam responded glumly.

"Sam's probably right," Carrie said quietly. "At least, that's what I feel in my heart."

"What do you feel?" Emma asked.

Carrie stared into the distance and tears filled her eyes, spilling silently onto her cheeks. "That Billy's going to die!" she whispered. "And that I did everything wrong! I never made love with him, and now I'll never get the chance, and I'm going to lose him! Oh, God, I can't stand it! I can't!"

Carrie broke down in inconsolable tears. All Emma and Sam could do was sit and hold her, and let her cry.

ELEVEN

Carrie picked her head up off the cafeteria table at the sound of Pres's voice gently calling her name.

"Wake up," Pres said gently. "You fell asleep."

"Where am I?" Carrie said groggily, until it all came back to her in one unending rush of horror and depression. She was still in the cafeteria, Billy was still upstairs in his room, and all the terrible events of the day had not been any kind of a dream at all.

At least Pres made it to the hospital, she thought, as she tried to pull herself awake. *That's good, anyway. Well, good in a comparative sort of way, I guess.*

"You know now?" Pres asked her. "Where you are, I mean."

"Unfortunately," she replied. "What time is it?"

"About two in the morning," Pres answered. "A little after, actually."

"Where is everyone else?" Carrie demanded. "Nothing happened to Billy, did it?" A moment of sheer terror turned Carrie's stomach upside down.

"Nothing happened to Billy," Pres assured her. "He's still asleep. Everyone else is in the main lounge upstairs. Emma and Sam are up there. Jay and Sly and me got here about an hour ago."

"I must have fallen asleep," Carrie said wearily. She felt a terrible pounding in her temples, and she rubbed her fingers over it.

"Hurts, huh?" Pres said softly. He got up and stood behind Carrie, gently rubbing her temples in a circular motion. "Better?"

Carrie nodded, her eyes closed. "But it doesn't feel right," she admitted. "I feel like I *should* be in physical pain." She opened her eyes. "I must have really crashed out, huh?"

Pres smiled a small smile. "I'll say," he whispered. "No one had the heart to wake you. Seemed like you needed your rest."

Carrie looked around. There was no one in the cafeteria except for herself, Pres, and a couple of tired-looking maintenance people washing the floor and wiping down tables.

"Have you seen him?" Carrie asked. "Did anything change?"

"Unh-uh," Pres answered, shaking his head. "He's asleep, too."

"But you heard—"

"Emma and Sam filled us in," Pres said quietly. "But that note you left us sort of summed it up, didn't it? We were so shocked. At first we thought it was some lame kind of joke—"

"No joke," Carrie replied.

"Yeah, obviously," Pres said. "But it doesn't seem real to me."

"Me, either," Carrie agreed. She stared hard at Pres. "It's like . . . it's like anything awful can happen to anyone at any minute—you know what I mean?"

Pres nodded.

"So, how are we supposed to live like that?" Carrie demanded.

Pres reached for Carrie's hand. "You just keep on, I guess," he said. "Dang, that sure sounds lame. I hate this."

"I hate this, too," Carrie agreed.

"Billy is the best friend I ever had," Pres said quietly. "He's always been there for me. He's . . . steady, you know? He's the one you never expect anything bad to happen to—"

"Yeah," Carrie agreed. "But it did."

Pres shook his head. "The world doesn't make any damn sense, Car. Why should something so awful happen to Sly, and now Billy? Why can't it happen to . . . to murderers or rapists?"

"I don't know," Carrie said. "I wish I did."

Pres rubbed his face wearily. "Maybe we're all just God's little cosmic joke or something."

"Or maybe we're all being tested, somehow?" Carrie suggested softly.

Pres managed a small smile. "I grew up in the 'Bible Belt.' My parents were very big into the church—they about died when I went into rock and roll and dropped out of college. They believe that God directly intervenes in our lives. They believe it with all their heart—"

"And you don't?" Carrie asked him.

Pres thought a minute. "I believe in God," he finally said. "'Cuz I know there is something bigger than me in this world. But beyond that . . . I just don't know. I mean, in a world where innocent people suffer, how can we say that God intervenes?"

"Maybe . . . well, maybe there's a reason, and we just don't understand it," Carrie said slowly. "Like, maybe we're all supposed to learn something from Sly getting sick—"

"Now, that is turkey turds to me," Pres replied. "What kind of God would do that to Sly so we could learn? Why Sly? Why Billy? Why?"

Pres's eyes filled up with tears, and Carrie put her arms around him. "I don't know," she said softly. "I don't know."

Finally he lifted his head. "Whew, sorry about that. I'm kinda undone, here."

"It's okay," Carrie said. "Me, too."

Pres took a deep breath. "Anyway, like I said, everyone's upstairs. Except Diana. She said she was busy."

"No great loss," Carrie answered honestly. "I wouldn't want her around, anyway."

"Never let it be said that I had something nasty to say about someone in the band," Pres commented, "but these are extenuating circumstances. I agree. You want coffee?"

"Sure," Carrie said, "I guess."

"There's a pot upstairs," Pres said. "Come on, let's go."

Carrie stood up from the table slowly and stretched out her stiffened limbs. Then she followed Pres through the quiet hospital corridors to a bank of elevators. They took one to the first floor lounge. There Emma, Sam, and Jay were sitting quietly together.

"Hey, girlfriend," Sam said listlessly, as Carrie approached.

"Where's Sly?" Pres asked.

"In Billy's room," Emma reported. "When Billy found out he was here, he said he wanted to talk to him. Since his family's not here, and he's so upset, the nurse on duty said Sly could visit for a while."

"He woke up!" Carrie cried.

"Just a few minutes ago," Jay said.

"I've got to see him," Carrie said, her voice getting a little frantic, her headache practically forgotten at the news.

Pres turned to her. "If Billy wants to talk to Sly alone, I think you should let him," he said gently. "It won't be but a minute, anyway."

Carrie thought about it, then nodded her head in agreement. She slumped down in one of the unoccupied chairs, as tired as she was when she fell asleep.

Emma came and sat in the chair next to her.

"You okay?" Emma asked.

"No," Carrie said honestly. "I'm not okay. I'm a nervous wreck." Then Carrie breathed in sharply. She remembered what she had been dreaming at the exact moment that Pres had awakened her, and the memory was a terrible thing to recall.

"What is it?" Emma asked. "You look like you just saw a ghost."

"Kind of," Carrie mumbled. "I just remembered the dream I had. It was the most horrible dream in the world."

"What?" Emma asked quietly.

"I dreamed I was at Billy's funeral," Carrie reported. "Everyone was there. And he sat up in his coffin and started crying."

"Oh, my God," Emma breathed, taken aback. "I'm sorry. It'll be okay, I know it will."

"I wish we did know that," Carrie said honestly. "But I appreciate the sentiment."

Just then Sly came back into the lounge. He looked more tired than Carrie had ever seen him before. In his plain white T-shirt, suede vest, and white painter's pants, she could see how thin and gaunt he had actually become.

Will Billy look like that in a month? Six months? A year? she asked herself.

"How is he?" she asked Sly.

Sly shrugged. "Freaked," he said. "He wants to talk to you. The nurse said it was okay."

Carrie got up. "I'm on my way," she declared.

"And he wants me to come back," Sly added. "With you. Now."

This time it was Carrie's turn to shrug. If Billy wanted to speak to Carrie and Sly together, that was okay with her. Just so long as she could see him!

She and Sly took the elevator to the second floor and walked down the long corridor to Billy's room. They passed empty rooms and rooms with patients in them, the nurses station, a room where someone was moaning in pain. Carrie winced.

Will Billy sound like that in a month? Six months? A year? she asked herself again.

They turned into Billy's room. Billy was now sitting up in bed, sipping some water out of a paper cup.

He doesn't look as bad as he did when we got here, Carrie realized. *He looks*

169

scared, yes, but somehow not quite as scared.

Carrie went to him and threw her arms around him, once again resolved to not let Billy see how upset she was. Sly just looked on as the two of them shared a fervent embrace.

"Sit down," Billy said finally. "Please." He motioned to the two vinyl chairs at the side of his bed. Sly sat down in one, and Carrie sat in the other.

"Sly and I had a chance to talk," Billy said.

"I know," Carrie answered.

"I thought he would understand what I'm going through," Billy explained, taking another sip of water.

"Did he?" Carrie asked.

"Kinda," Billy said. "But it didn't help much."

"That's what I told him would happen," Sly explained. "He didn't believe me."

"I do now." Billy sighed. "I never really thought about dying before."

"Neither did I," Sly said.

"But I've sure done a lot of thinking about it tonight," Billy said.

Carrie sat silently. *What could I possibly add to this?* she thought to herself. *I don't have a terminal disease. I'm not going to die soon. But maybe I am. Who knows? Who ever knows?*

"We talked about regrets," Billy continued. "Sly said I should talk about that with you."

"If you get them out in the open, they're not so tough to deal with. And that," Sly said, "is my cue to leave." Without saying another word, he got up and left the hospital room, leaving Carrie and Billy alone.

Billy looked at Carrie. "You start," he said quietly.

"I really don't want to do this," Carrie answered, fighting back her tears. "It's morbid. You're acting like you're already dead."

"That's kind of how I feel," Billy responded.

"That attitude is not going to get you anywhere," Carrie answered sharply. "So, just stop it!"

"I can't," Billy said. "I feel how I feel."

"Defeatist, you mean?"

"No, pissed off!" Billy yelled.

"Well, me, too!" Carrie yelled back, jumping up.

They stared at each other, and finally both of them smiled.

"Now, can we talk?" Billy asked in a normal voice.

Carrie nodded and sat back down.

"Well, I regret that we never made love," Billy stated.

"We still can—"

"I don't think so, Car," Billy interrupted. "Your boyfriend is going to be some guy who throws up from chemotherapy and is bald besides! How's that going to feel?"

"Billy," Carrie whispered fervently, "as long as you fight, as long as you live, it's going to feel fine. Wonderful. All I care about is that you live!"

"That's easy to say when I'm lying here looking normal—"

"Oh, Billy, don't you have any faith in me at all?" Carrie cried. "Do you think I'll only love you if . . . if you have hair? Or if you're healthy?"

"I don't know," Billy said honestly, his voice cracking.

"I do," Carrie replied. She put her hand over her heart. "I could never, ever leave you. No matter what. I love you."

Billy's eyes filled with tears. "Car, I'm so scared. And I know I'm acting like a big baby—" He managed a small, ragged laugh. "Hey, you are definitely seeing me at my worst!"

"I can deal," Carrie said, grabbing his hand and holding on tight.

"So can I," Billy said. "Well, at least, I think I can deal."

"Everyone's here for you," Carrie told him.

"Yeah, that's what Sly said," Billy murmured. "I can't believe it."

Carrie was surprised. "How can you say that? They love you."

"That means a lot," Billy admitted. "That means everything." He raised Carrie's hand to his lips and kissed it. "So, do you have any regrets?"

"I regret that we didn't make love, too," she admitted. "And I regret that we didn't get to spend more time together, just the two of us, no one else."

Billy squeezed her hand.

"But, Billy, we'll have those chances again!" Carrie said fervently. "I believe that with all my heart. I believe you're going to get better."

"I'm going to try and believe it, too," Billy said, gulping hard.

"Did talking to Sly really help you?" Carrie asked him.

Billy nodded. "He's been through the mill. He told me about when he found out."

"It was in Maryland, right?" Carrie asked.

Billy shook his head. "Nope," he replied. "It was more than a year ago."

"You're kidding," Carrie marveled. "And he kept it from everyone?"

"He was afraid of what people would think."

"How horrible," Carrie said. "What a huge burden." She shook her head. "God, it's so unfair, isn't it? I mean, if you get sick with cancer, you're not afraid people will judge you. But if you get AIDS, you try to hide it from even the people who love you. . . ."

"Yeah," Billy agreed. "Anyway, I'm lucky he's here. It helps a lot."

"I'm glad," Carrie said softly.

Billy smiled at her. "Do you know how much I love you?"

"I hope," Carrie said, "it's as much as I love you."

Carrie intended to sit there until Billy fell asleep again and then go back to where her friends were waiting in the lounge. But what she intended wasn't what happened. About the same time Billy fell asleep, Carrie did, too. And they slept there, hand in hand, bound by love, ready to face whatever they had to face together.

TWELVE

"Miss?"

Carrie opened her eyes. Standing at the door of Billy's room was a nurse and behind her was Diana De Witt. The nurse walked over to the bed. "You weren't supposed to stay all night," she whispered. "But I didn't have the heart to wake you. I'm a big fan of Flirting With Danger," she said.

"Thanks," Carrie whispered, sitting up. She'd been asleep with her head on Billy's chest. She could see the rays of dawn coming in through the window.

"Hi," Diana said quietly, as the nurse left the room.

"What do you want?" Carrie asked

bluntly. She looked at her watch. It was six o'clock in the morning.

"You look awful," Diana said, not moving.

Carrie stretched and heard her back crack. "Thanks for that news bulletin, Diana. Now get lost before you wake Billy."

"I . . ." Diana began.

Carrie got up and walked to the door. "What?" she asked again impatiently. "You're here to gloat? You had a free minute between dates?"

Billy mumbled something in his sleep and moved around in bed. "Come out into the hall," she whispered to Diana. "I don't want to wake him."

Diana dutifully followed Carrie into the hall. Carrie closed Billy's door behind her.

"I came to see Billy," Diana finally said.

"Great, you just saw him," Carrie replied. "Bye."

"You don't need to be so nasty," Diana said. "I didn't have to come at all."

"You know, I'm in no mood to be nice to you and I'm in no mood to put up with you," Carrie told Diana. It felt good to let some of her anger loose on a person she so disliked.

"Look, I know you hate me," Diana said.

"Aren't you the rocket scientist?" Carrie marveled, enjoying her venom.

Diana held her ground. "I care about Billy," she said evenly.

"Sure," Carrie snorted. "I guess that's why you rushed here last night with everyone else who cares about him."

"I didn't come here last night because—"

"You were busy," Carrie filled in for her. "Fine. Who cares?"

"I wasn't busy," Diana said in a low voice. "I was scared."

Carrie just stared at her.

Diana looked down at the floor and then raised her eyes to Carrie. "I had a little sister who died of leukemia a long time ago. Her name was Cassandra—Cassie. I was five years old when she died. She was three."

"I'm sorry," Carrie managed stiffly.

"I'm not asking you to feel sorry for me, okay?" Diana said. "I'm just telling you what happened."

Carrie nodded.

Diana pushed her hair back from her face. "I . . . I really care about Billy," she said in a low voice. "He's always been totally decent to me."

"He's decent to everybody," Carrie replied.

Diana fiddled with the clasp on her purse. "Once last summer, I was at a party. He was there, too. You were working, I think. Anyway, I got drunk—really polluted," Diana continued, still staring at the clasp on her purse, "and I guess I ended up in a bedroom with some guys I didn't know . . ."

"Diana, please, I'm not interested in hearing this—"

"Just let me finish," Diana said earnestly. "And these guys turned out to be real jerks. They were all over me, and I was trying to get away, but I was so out of it I couldn't fight them off too well. I was scared—really, really scared." She looked Carrie straight in the eye. "And then Billy was there. And he got rid of the guys. And he got me some coffee and well . . . he took care of me. Afterward he took me home."

My God, I don't believe it, Carrie marveled. *There are actually real tears in Diana De Witt's eyes. . . .*

"I asked Billy not to tell anyone," Diana continued, "and he never did." Her jaw was set in a hard line. "I would have done anything for Billy that night. Anything," she repeated, to make sure Carrie got her point. "Billy knew it. And he didn't make a move on me. He just took care of me. And he never told a soul."

Carrie reached out and lightly touched Diana's arm. "Thanks for telling me."

"You're really lucky, Carrie," Diana said, "to have a guy like that."

Carrie nodded, although at the moment she didn't feel too lucky.

Diana shook her hair back, shaking off Carrie's touch at the same time. "So, anyway," Diana said. "Can I go in and see him?"

"I don't want to wake him up," Carrie replied.

"Oh, okay," Diana agreed, shifting her weight. "Well, will you tell him I was here?"

"Why don't you just wait in the lounge with everyone else?" Carrie suggested. "Then you can see him when he wakes up."

"I don't think they want me there," Diana said in a low voice.

"Look, you're part of the band," Carrie told her. "And this is a time for the band to stick together."

"Yeah," Diana agreed, though she sounded unsure.

"It's fine," Carrie assured her. "Really."

Diana took a deep breath. She seemed to shake off her insecurity with a toss of her curls. "Yeah, cool," she decided, sounding like the old Diana. "So, listen, you won't tell anyone about this little conversation, will you?"

"No, I won't," Carrie promised. "But what I want to know, now that I see you're an actual human being, how come you spend all your time acting like such a bitch?"

"Hey, I've got a rep to maintain," Diana coolly threw back over her shoulder as she strode away.

I'll never understand her, Carrie thought to herself as she tiptoed back into Billy's room. She looked down at Billy's sleeping face. *He is so gorgeous,* she thought to herself. *And I love him so much.*

She sat in the same chair she'd been in before and carefully took Billy's hand again. "You are a wonderful person, Billy Sampson," she whispered to him. "Even Diana knows you are."

Then she laid her head back down on Billy's chest, and listened again to the sound of his beating heart.

Carrie was awakened by Dr. Lowe's footsteps coming into the room later that morning. He nodded at her quickly, then pulled a chair up to the other side of Billy's bed.

"Billy," Dr. Lowe said in a loud voice.

Carrie's heart began to hammer in her

chest. *The doctor sounds so insistent,* Carrie realized. *It must be terrible news.*

"Wake up, Billy," Dr. Lowe said, speaking even louder.

"Huh?" Billy said, waking up with a start. His eyes met Dr. Lowe's, then he shifted his gaze to Carrie. She grabbed his hand and held it tight.

"Put your clothes on," Dr. Lowe ordered.

"What?"

What's this all about? It must be the bone marrow biopsy—he must have to change buildings, Carrie thought.

"Put your clothes on," Dr. Lowe repeated. "You're going home."

"I'm . . . what?" Billy asked, completely confused.

"We just got your lab results back," Dr. Lowe said, a big smile spreading over his tired face. "Your blood levels are normal."

"Normal," Billy repeated dully.

"Normal," Dr. Lowe repeated. "Someone at the lab screwed up your blood sample last week. There's gonna be hell to pay. But meanwhile, you're fine."

"Fine," Billy repeated. "I'm fine."

"You got it," Dr. Lowe said. "I've already called Doctor Mullins. Sorry if you had a rough night last night."

Billy sat up straighter in bed. "Wait a second. I'm fine? Someone screwed up my tests? You're telling me I'm *fine?*" His voice was rising higher and higher.

"That's what I'm telling you," the doctor said.

"I went through all of this for *nothing?*" Billy asked.

"Would you rather I told you you were seriously ill so you could have gone through it for something?" Dr. Lowe asked ironically.

A slow grin spread over Billy's face. "No," he said. He turned to Carrie.

"I'm numb," Carrie whispered.

"I'm fine," he told her, as if to convince himself.

"Thank you, God!" Carrie screamed, and she flung herself across Billy.

"Well, I'll leave you two alone now," the doctor said. "It was a pleasure to be able to bring you such good news."

"Thanks," Billy said, then anxiety flitted across his face and he grabbed the doctor's hand. "Wait a sec. What if this is another mistake? I mean, what if these results are screwed up? I've gotta know—I can't go through this again."

"I am certain you are fine," Dr. Lowe assured Billy. "The first tests were done the same day on someone else, who really does have leukemia. We've found that person and repeated his tests. You're totally in the clear."

"And some other poor slob has leukemia," Billy said.

The doctor nodded.

"It could just as easily have been me," Billy mused.

The doctor nodded again. "There but for the grace of God go I," he added.

"Thanks, again, Doctor Lowe," Billy said, shaking the doctor's hand.

"Have a long, healthy, wonderful life," Dr. Lowe said, and he walked away.

Carrie was snuggled next to Billy in the hospital bed, hugging him hard.

"Hey, I bet this is against regulations, big-time," Billy told her with a laugh.

"Ask me if I care," Carrie told him. She

rolled over on top of him. "I love you!" she cried, and pelted his face with kisses. Then she jumped up. "Hey, I have to go tell everyone!" She leaned over and kissed him again. "I'll be right back!"

Carrie ran to the elevator, filled with so much energy she thought she could take off and fly. When she got to the lounge everyone was there, some sleeping, some reading, some staring out the window. They all turned to look at her when she ran into the room.

"He's fine," Carrie whispered.

They all stared at her.

"Fine?" Pres finally said.

Carrie nodded. "Fine! Healthy! Wonderful!"

Diana stood up. "He doesn't have leukemia?"

"No!" Carrie cried. "There was a lab mix-up!"

"Are they sure?" Sly asked.

"Totally!" Carrie replied.

Everyone was still too stunned to move.

"I say we go attack that malingering brat!" Sam finally squealed.

Everyone laughed, and all together

they ran to the elevator and down the hall to Billy's room. They ignored the nurses who tried to stop them and all pushed into Billy's room.

And then, all at once, they jumped on Billy's bed, a wild tangle of arms and legs.

"What you won't do for attention!" Sam yelled, tickling Billy in the ribs.

"Hey, you guys are heavy!" Billy yelled, but he was laughing so hard he could hardly get the words out.

"Oof, those are my ribs," Jay said, pushing Diana, who fell off the bed and onto the floor, laughing hysterically.

"Excuse me," a stern voice called from the doorway, "but this is completely against regulations!" The tall, thin nurse who stood there was practically quivering with indignation.

"It's a fraternity initiation," Jay invented. "We had to see how many people we could fit on one hospital bed!"

"Well, you'll have to leave at once!" the nurse cried.

"We'll be happy to leave," Billy said.

"Not you!" the nurse replied, aghast. "You're the patient!"

"Not anymore," Billy announced, a huge grin spread across his face. "I am outta here!"

THIRTEEN

"What *are* you wearing?" Carrie asked Sam, laughing incredulously.

"Next to nothing," Sam replied truthfully, looking down at her new bikini, a hot pink crocheted string with a couple of little crocheted pieces that covered—just barely—what had to be covered. Sam had her hair skewered haphazardly on the top of her head with two pink chopstick-looking things, and she had on pink lipstick that matched the bikini. Over the swimsuit she wore a see-through shirt covered in pink hearts.

It was later that evening, and they were all at the beach for an impromptu bonfire and picnic. After the terrible scare over Billy, everyone was in a fabulous mood. Word had spread quickly that Billy was okay, and about a dozen other friends were on the beach, standing around the bonfire that Howie Lawrence had built. Molly Mason sat next to Howie while he roasted her a hotdog over the fire. Darcy Laken was playing Frisbee with Jay Bailey and two of the day-shift waitresses from the Play Café.

"Well, next to nothing looks great on you," Carrie told her, "though I don't know where you put food." She eyed Sam's practically concave tummy.

"Hey, I look at it this way—" Sam replied, grabbing a handful of chips off the picnic table they'd set up "—the Lord giveth, and the Lord taketh away."

Carrie looked down the beach at Billy, standing near the shoreline with Sly. "That's the truth, huh?" she agreed softly.

Sam sat down on a beach chair and drew her knees up to her chin. "I don't mind telling you, Car, I was so scared for Billy. . . ."

"Yeah," Carrie murmured. She looked

back at Sam. "It just didn't seem real, you know?"

"Well, fortunately it turned out to *not* be real," Sam pointed out. She reached for another handful of chips. "It kind of makes you wonder, though, doesn't it? I mean, is it really so easy for labs to mix up tests?" Sam shuddered and reached into the cooler for a Coke.

"I don't know," Carrie replied. "I asked my parents about it—they're both doctors, you know. My mom said 'Well, honey, it's rare, but it happens.'"

"That's not a lot of comfort," Sam said. She looked out at Billy and Sly. "But I guess that's the least of anyone's worries, huh?"

Carrie sat down next to Sam. "I am a terrible person," she blurted out.

Sam looked at her. "You? Saint Carrie?"

"I am," Carrie insisted. "When I looked over there at Sly and Billy just now, I thought to myself, 'I am so glad it's Sly that's sick, and not Billy.'"

Sam made a face. "That is kind of gruesome."

"I know," Carrie agreed. "It's like I want to make some kind of bargain with God. Like, well, you zapped one of my friends, so you can't zap the other."

"I don't think it works that way," Sam said, stretching her legs out and flexing her toes.

"I don't think so, either," Carrie said, standing up. She reached into a paper bag and set out some more of the food. "It's funny, isn't it, Sam, how we only seem to have this God conversation when something really awful happens."

Sam jumped up. "This is all too heavy. We're supposed to be celebrating!"

Carrie gave her a sad look. "Sly can't celebrate."

"Well, he's alive, isn't he?" Sam pointed out.

"For the moment," Carrie replied.

"So, for the moment, let's celebrate," Sam said. She grabbed a marshmallow and popped it into her mouth. "I don't suppose Pres is here yet."

Carrie shook her head no. "And neither is Emma, but she told me she might have to put the kids to bed before she could come."

Sam shivered as the sun began to set and the temperature fell. "Well, I wish Pres would hurry up and get here so I could put some clothes on."

Carrie laughed. "Oh, you're freezing your butt off for him, huh?"

Sam gave Carrie a disdainful look. "You didn't think it was for your benefit, did you?"

Carrie laughed again. "Hardly."

"Uh-oh," Sam muttered as she caught sight of Diana sauntering toward them. "Trouble heading this way. Red alert! red alert!"

"Hi," Diana said, reaching into the cooler for a drink.

"Hi," Carrie replied.

"You need help setting stuff up?" Diana asked.

Carrie stared at Diana, her mouth open. "Excuse me, did you just offer to help?"

"Gee, I could have sworn I did," Diana confirmed.

"So, where's the zinger?" Sam asked her. "Where's the bitchy follow-up?"

Diana shrugged and pushed some curls back from her face.

"Thanks, but the food's all out now," Carrie finally told her.

"Oh, okay," Diana replied. She looked down the beach at Billy and Sly, who still appeared to be deep in conversation.

"I wonder what they're talking about," Carrie mused.

"Probably life and death and all that big stuff," Sam guessed.

Diana laughed. "I was just over there. They're arguing about which is the greatest rock band of all time—the Doors, the Rolling Stones or the Beatles."

"You're kidding," Sam said.

"Nope," Diana replied. "And before that they were talking about the drum riff on 'Tough Enough.' Billy thinks it needs to be a little tighter."

Carrie smiled. "So, we're over here thinking deep thoughts, and they're hanging out."

"Basically," Diana agreed. She looked over at Carrie and Sam. "I took a walk with Sly earlier and he said to me, 'Diana, I'm not dying of AIDS. I am living with AIDS.'"

Sam bit her lower lip contemplatively. "Unreal. And I get all bent out of shape if I catch a cold."

Diana eyed Sam's outfit. "Well, you're gonna catch more than a cold in that tacky little outfit."

Sam rolled her eyes. "Ah, there's the Diana we know and loathe."

Diana shrugged. "I'm just telling you the truth, Sam. And if the truth hurts, that's your problem." She reached for a chip. "But if you're wearing that little ensemble to impress Pres when he gets here, I'll let you in on a little secret." She leaned toward Sam. "There is nothing more pathetic than a girl who is trying too hard."

"Well, we sure appreciate that news flash," Carrie told her sarcastically.

Diana sighed and shook her head at Carrie. "Between your hiding in your baggy jeans and T-shirts and Sam's pathetically undressing to flaunt her lack of assets, I'm amazed that *either* of you *ever* get a guy!"

"Oh, yeah?" Sam shot back. "You get every guy. For one night, that is."

Diana gave Sam a cool smile. "Well, whatever I do is on my terms, not theirs."

Carrie leaned toward Diana. "And now I'll let you in on a little secret, Diana. One-night stands are dumb. Really, really dumb. You can die like that."

"Oh, well," Diana said breezily. "When your number's up, I guess you're number's up!"

Carrie folded her arms. "I guess you think it can't happen to you. But just remember, that's what Sly thought, too."

Some of the color drained out of Diana's face. "Look, the guys I'm with are not lowlifes—"

Carrie made a sound of exasperation deep in her throat. "Don't you get it?" she cried. "It doesn't have anything to do with . . . with being a lowlife. Anybody can get AIDS. Anybody! Even you."

Diana took a deep breath. "Yeah, like you'd care."

Carrie stared her down.

"It doesn't matter whether I'd care or not, Diana." Carrie finally said in a low voice. "I hope *you* care."

For once, Diana seemed to have no comeback. She just turned and walked away.

"I don't believe it," Sam marveled. "You just gave Diana I-drool-over-anything-that-zips-at-the-crotch De Witt a lecture on safe sex!"

"*Safer*," Carrie corrected. "There is no really safe sex." She noticed a car pulling into the lot nearest them. "That's the Hewitts' car—Emma's here."

Sam watched Emma get out of the car and Pres get out the other side. She gave Carrie a look of alarm. "She came with Pres?"

"Probably she just gave him a ride," Carrie said.

Sam looked around frantically. "Where's my sweatshirt? I look like an idiot standing around in this." She grabbed someone's sweatshirt off a beach chair and struggled into it just as Emma and Pres walked over. But she was in such a rush that she was trying to poke her head through an arm hole and wound up hopelessly tangled.

"Hi, sorry I'm late," Emma said. "I didn't think Katie would ever get to sleep!"

"Hey," Pres said in his lazy voice, eyeing Sam caught inside the navy-blue sweatshirt. "You under there?"

"Oh, sure," Sam mumbled, finally righting the sweatshirt. Her head popped through the neckline and she shook her hair out. "So, here I am! And here are the two of you! Together!" she said a bit too gaily.

"My bike broke down near Emma's house," Pres explained. "I walked it part of the way and then she gave me a ride."

"So I see," Sam said, trying to not sound as betrayed as she felt. She grabbed her jeans and pulled them on.

Everyone was quiet for a moment.

"So, this is really nice," Emma finally said.

"Where's Billy?" Pres asked, looking around.

"Behind ya, buddy," Billy said, coming up on the other side of the group. He gave Pres a hug. "Glad to see you."

"How you feelin', man?" Pres asked.

"I feel . . . like a million," Billy said, a huge grin spreading across his handsome face.

Carrie quietly picked up her camera and clicked off a shot of him.

"There's nothing like thinking you're gonna die to make you appreciate living," Billy continued.

"Actually, there's nothing like *knowing* you're going to die to make you appreciate living," Sly said, ambling over to them.

Everyone looked at him, then looked away.

"Hey, that was not meant as a downer!" he yelled. "If everyone is going to mope at this bash, I am outta here!" He reached into the cooler for a soda. "So, someone crank up the tunes!"

Billy hit Sly on the arm. "Yeah, you probably only want to hear the Doors, since you think they were so hot."

"Actually, I think the Flirts are hot," Sly replied. "Stick in one of our tapes!"

Emma complied and the sounds of their demo of "Wild Child" filled the air.

"Damn, we're good," Sly said with satisfaction.

"Hi, everyone!" a young male voice called to them. They all turned around, and there was Ian Templeton, running toward them from the parking lot. Becky Jacobs followed close behind.

"What are you doing here?" Carrie asked. She peered toward the parking lot, but it was dark now and she couldn't really see. "And how did you get here?"

"Becky's dad drove us," Ian explained. "I told him it was imperative that we get down here," he added seriously.

Becky threw her arms around Billy. "I'm so glad you're okay!"

Billy hugged her quickly and let her go. "Thanks," he replied.

"Hey, what about the chicken pox?" Emma asked them.

"We're almost cured," Ian replied. "The doctor even said we could go out 'cause we're not contagious anymore."

"Excuse me, Becky, but no one invited you to this party," Sam told her charge.

Becky looked insulted. "Excuse me, but this is a free beach, last time I heard." She turned to Sly. "You have AIDS, right?"

"Gee, neat segue, Beck," Sam said under her breath.

"Right," Sly confirmed easily.

"Well, listen," Becky continued, "a lot of little kids think they can get it by, like, drinking from a drinking fountain you drank from. I mean, it is really dumb!"

"So that's why Becky and I thought of having the Zits do a fundraiser for AIDS—you know—to educate kids and stuff," Ian continued earnestly.

"The Zits have a following?" Sam asked dryly.

"Of course," Ian replied with dignity. "I took a survey, and we are the most popular band under sixteen on the island."

"You're the only band under sixteen on the island," Sam pointed out.

Becky looked ready to cry. "Look, you can put us down if you want to, but this is important. I know kids my age who are having sex. They all think nothing bad can ever happen to them. You think I want one of my friends to get sick?"

"I'm sorry," Sam said, truly contrite. "Really."

"We're planning to debut our new single, 'Chicken Pox Rox,' at a kids night at the Play Café next week," Ian said eagerly. "And we want to make it an AIDS fundraiser, like the Flirts did."

"Your new single?" Sly asked. "You guys got a record deal?"

"Well, maybe it will be our first single when we do get a record deal," Ian clarified. "I think we're really close. So, what do you think about my idea?

"Our idea," Becky corrected.

"I think that's a great idea," Sly told Ian.

"Great," Ian replied casually, trying to look cool. "So, I'll plan the gig."

Carrie quickly snapped a shot of Ian, then as the group continued talking, she clicked away.

"Hey, Madam Photographer," Billy said, coming up behind Carrie and nuzzling her neck.

"Mmmm, that feels good," she said softly, leaning into Billy's caress.

"How about we take a walk down the beach?"

"Love to," Carrie replied. "Be back eventually," Carrie called to her friends over her shoulder as Billy took her hand.

They walked away in silence.

"Emma showed up with Pres," Carrie finally said.

"Oh, yeah?" Billy asked.

"Is there something going on there?" Carrie asked him.

"Not that I know of," Billy replied. "I mean, he thinks Emma is great, but who doesn't?"

"It would kill Sam, you know," Carrie said, "if there was anything between them."

Billy draped his arm around Carrie's shoulder. "Right now, babe, I'd just as soon let all of them sort out their own stuff—you know what I mean?"

Carrie nodded and snuggled next to Billy. "You're right."

Billy picked up a shell and hurled it out into the water. "I used to do that with rocks when I was a kid—you know—

skim them across the water. Ever do that?"

"I never could get the rock to hop," Carrie remembered. "My brothers always could and I couldn't."

"Poor Carrie," Billy teased. "Living with that kind of emotional scar."

Carrie poked him in the ribs. "You can be replaced, you know."

Billy stopped walking and turned to her. "Can I?"

Carrie stared up at him, the moonlight shining on his handsome face. "No," she replied. "I guess not."

Billy cupped Carrie's face and gently kissed her. "Did I mention that I love you, even if you can't skim a stone?"

"Big of you," Carrie whispered, burrowing her face in Billy's neck.

Billy held her against him. "I feel . . . I feel like I'm being given another chance, you know what I mean? Like maybe I had this scare for a reason."

Carrie nodded and pressed herself even closer.

"When I wake up tomorrow morning, I

can say 'Yo, Billy, you are healthy.' Sly can't say that. Not ever again."

"I know," Carrie whispered.

Billy held her at arms' length. "I told Sly I felt guilty," he told her, searching her face with his eyes. "I mean, like I was using what happened to him to appreciate my life more—it didn't feel right. But he just told me he was glad. That's all he said. That he was glad."

"Oh, Billy . . ." Carrie murmured, and she wrapped her arms around his neck. "Maybe Sly feels like . . . like he's glad something good can come from something so awful. Couldn't that be it?"

Billy nodded. Tears came to his eyes and he brushed them away quickly. "It just makes me want to live, you know?" he said. "Not hold back, go for everything . . ."

"I know. . . ."

"And to me," Billy continued, "everything is the band and you. And not necessarily in that order."

Carrie raised her face to kiss Billy on the lips.

"You know, if the band gets a deal, if we

become big stars, it won't mean anything if I don't have you," Billy told her passionately.

They kissed again and Carrie lost herself in the wonderful feeling of being in Billy's arms, of knowing he was healthy and knowing he loved her as much as she loved him.

"When I thought I might die, Car," Billy said, holding her against his chest, "I thought a lot about us. I thought about the future, you know? And the saddest thing of all to me was that we wouldn't have a chance to get married, to have kids, to have a life together."

Carrie's heart sped up in her chest. "We've never talked about things like that."

"I know," Billy replied. "Because it always seemed like we have forever. But we don't." He stared into Carrie's eyes. "In the hospital I woke up once in the middle of the night. And you were there, sleeping on my chest. And you were holding my hand. And I realized right then that nothing was more important than you and me. Nothing."

"I love you, Billy," Carrie whispered.

A small smile played at his lips. "How much?"

Carrie looked up at the sky. "More than all the stars shining up there," she said. "More than all the stars shining up there times infinity." She grinned at him. "I bet you can't top that, huh?"

"I can, too," he said, and pulled her close. Then he kissed her until there was no beach, no stars in the sky, not even infinity to think about.

There was only the two of them, and it was everything.

SUNSET ISLAND MAILBOX

Dear Readers,

I want to share with you an incredible letter that I received from a very special young woman. She was kind enough and brave enough to say that I could print her letter. I was deeply affected by it and I think you will be too. This is such a tough time to be a teen, and pregnancy is one of the most important issues going. Please send me your reactions and thoughts!

Ashley White of Loyall, Kentucky, and lots of others want to know what's going on with the movie version of <u>Sunset Island</u>. My husband, Jeff (you know, the guy all the books are dedicated to!), produces my work for stage and film and he is working very hard to get something going. I promise to keep you posted. But believe me, Hollywood is nuts and everything out there seems to take forever!

Great photos arrived recently from Elizabeth Good of Kingston, Nova Scotia, Robin Herenda of Berwin, Pennsylvania, and lots more. I just love it when you send me pictures. This week I got photos of Lysmeyaki Turis of Selanger, Malaysia, with her three best friends and fellow <u>Sunset</u> fans. (Isn't it cool to know they're reading <u>Sunset</u> in Malaysia?) Also from Carrie Stone of Jenks, Oklahoma, and her three best friends, who are all <u>Sunset</u> fans. You guys are all over the planet—the coolest!

I had a great birthday recently (in October). Thanks to all of you who sent me birthday cards. It was so thoughtful! I really appreciated it! I love to hear from you out there—what's going on in your lives, what you think of the books, what you're concerned about, and how we can make <u>Sunset Island</u> even better. After all, I write them for you.

Remember, I'll keep writing as long as you keep reading. And I do answer each and every letter. You'll definitely hear from me!

See you on the island!

Best—

Cherie Bennett

Cherie Bennett
c/o General Licensing Company
24 West 25th Street
New York, New York 10010.

All letters become property of the publisher.

Dear Cherie,

Hi, my name is Rae. I've read all your books, and I think they're pretty terrific. Which of course you already know, I'm sure. I'm probably not part of the usual age group who reads your books. You see I'm twenty-two.

I got pregnant when I was seventeen and in the middle of my senior year of high school. I did finish school, but I never got married (I felt I was too young). It made me realize my son's sperm donor (father) really wasn't so great after all. Anyway, I always wanted to go to school in New York to be a fashion designer, but I never made it.

That's why I like your books so much, they sort of let me know what going to college would have been like, with no responsibility but for yourself, and the freedom to choose to do what you want to do.

I was thinking, maybe you could write a book where a friend of Sam, Emma and Carrie's gets pregnant and actually keeps the baby! A lot of teenage girls are getting pregnant because they think it will make their boyfriends stay with them. Unfortunately this is not always true. Maybe you could talk about all the changes and responsibilities that come with having a baby. All the things you miss out on. Becoming a parent is a very hard thing to do, and it's even harder when you are young, and didn't plan for a baby.

I know you've taken a stand, since Sam and Emma are still virgins and Carrie has slept only with Josh. But maybe you can tell all the teens who read your books that sex isn't worth getting pregnant, or getting VD, which can make you sterile, or dying (of AIDS).

If you get pregnant your life changes drastically. No more slumber parties, no more going out whenever you want, guys tend to stay away because they think you are desperate, and it's too much for them to deal with. And you actually have a little life you have to protect and nurture.

Even though I have my parents, it's still lonely. They're real strict with us, and they don't let me go out a whole lot (thank goodness they let me live at home and didn't kick me out!). A lot of my friends disappeared after I got pregnant. I guess I wasn't so much fun anymore. So looking back, it just wasn't worth it. Hindsight is always 20/20.

Yours truly,
Rae Petermann
Rio Rancho, New Mexico

SUNSET ISLAND ™ *HEATS UP AFTER DARK*

Darcy Laken is a beautiful, street-smart eighteen-year-old befriended by Emma, Carrie, and Sam in *Sunset Scandal*. She lives on the *other* side of Sunset Island–in an old and foreboding house on a hill where she works for the eccentric Mason family. When Darcy and Molly Mason find themselves in danger, Darcy gets a premonition about who is responsible. But when she asks for help from the cute guy who is threatening to steal her heart, he doesn't believe her!

__*SUNSET AFTER DARK*   0-425-13772-4/$3.50
__*SUNSET AFTER MIDNIGHT* 0-425-13799-6/$3.50
__*SUNSET AFTER HOURS*   0-425-13666-3/$3.50

MORE ADVENTURES. . .
SAM, EMMA, AND CARRIE

__*SUNSET SURF*   0-425-13937-9/$3.99
__*SUNSET DECEPTIONS*   0-425-13905-0/$3.99
__*SUNSET ON THE ROAD*   0-425-13932-8/$3.99
__*SUNSET EMBRACE*   0-425-13840-2/$3.50
__*SUNSET WISHES*   0-425-13812-7/$3.99
__*SUNSET TOUCH*   0-425-13708-2/$3.99
__*SUNSET WEDDING*   0-425-13982-4/$3.99

Payable in U.S. funds. No cash orders accepted. Postage & handling: $1.75 for one book, 75¢ for each additional. Maximum postage $5.50. Prices, postage and handling charges may change without notice. Visa, Amex, MasterCard call 1-800-788-6262, ext. 1, refer to ad # 439

Or, check above books   Bill my: ☐ Visa   ☐ MasterCard   ☐ Amex
and send this order form to: (expires)
The Berkley Publishing Group   Card#_____
390 Murray Hill Pkwy., Dept. B   ($15 minimum)
East Rutherford, NJ 07073   Signature_____
Please allow 6 weeks for delivery.   Or enclosed is my: ☐ check   ☐ money order

Name_____   Book Total $_____

Address_____   Postage & Handling $_____

City_____   Applicable Sales Tax $_____
                                 (NY, NJ, PA, CA, GST Can.)
State/ZIP_____   Total Amount Due $_____

Read how Carrie, Emma, and Sam
began their Sunset Island escapades.
Love. Laughter. Romance. Dreams come
true, and friendships last a lifetime.

SUNSET ISLAND ™

CHERIE BENNETT

When Emma, Sam, and Carrie spend the summer working
as au pairs on a resort island, they quickly become allies
in adventure!

__SUNSET ISLAND	0-425-12969-1/$3.99
__SUNSET KISS	0-425-12899-7/$3.50
__SUNSET DREAMS	0-425-13070-3/$3.50
__SUNSET FAREWELL	0-425-12772-9/$3.50
__SUNSET REUNION	0-425-13318-4/$3.50
__SUNSET SECRETS	0-425-13319-2/$3.99

Payable in U.S. funds. No cash orders accepted. Postage & handling: $1.75 for one book, 75¢
for each additional. Maximum postage $5.50. Prices, postage and handling charges may
change without notice. Visa, Amex, MasterCard call 1-800-788-6262, ext. 1, refer to ad # 366

Or, check above books and send this order form to:	Bill my: ☐ Visa ☐ MasterCard ☐ Amex	
The Berkley Publishing Group	Card#_____	(expires)
390 Murray Hill Pkwy., Dept. B		($15 minimum)
East Rutherford, NJ 07073	Signature_____	
Please allow 6 weeks for delivery.	Or enclosed is my: ☐ check ☐ money order	
Name_____	Book Total $_____	
Address_____	Postage & Handling $_____	
City_____	Applicable Sales Tax $_____ (NY, NJ, PA, CA, GST Can.)	
State/ZIP_____	Total Amount Due $_____	

Nicholas Pine's
TERROR ACADEMY

Welcome to Central Academy.
It's like any other high school on the outside.
But inside, terror is in a class by itself.

LIGHTS OUT	0-425-13709-0/$3.50
STALKER	0-425-13814-3/$3.50
SIXTEEN CANDLES	0-425-13841-0/$3.50
SPRING BREAK	0-425-13969-7/$3.50
THE NEW KID	0-425-13970-0/$3.50
STUDENT BODY	0-425-13983-2/$3.50
NIGHT SCHOOL	0-425-14151-9/$3.50
SCIENCE PROJECT	0-425-14152-7/$3.50
THE PROM	0-425-14153-5/$3.50
THE IN-CROWD	0-425-14307-4/$3.50
(coming in June)	

Payable in U.S. funds. No cash orders accepted. Postage & handling: $1.75 for one book, 75¢ for each additional. Maximum postage $5.50. Prices, postage and handling charges may change without notice. Visa, Amex, MasterCard call 1-800-788-6262, ext. 1, refer to ad # 453

Or, check above books   **Bill my:** ☐ Visa ☐ MasterCard ☐ Amex _____
and send this order form to: (expires)
The Berkley Publishing Group   Card#_____
390 Murray Hill Pkwy., Dept. B   ($15 minimum)
East Rutherford, NJ 07073   Signature_____
Please allow 6 weeks for delivery.   Or enclosed is my: ☐ check ☐ money order

Name_____ Book Total $_____

Address_____ Postage & Handling $_____

City_____ Applicable Sales Tax $_____
                                        (NY, NJ, PA, CA, GST Can.)
State/ZIP_____ Total Amount Due $_____